SKULL AND SIDECAR

SKULL & SIDECAR

A NOVEL

By Kristen Hall-Geisler

PRACTICAL
FOX

Portland, Oregon

Skull and Sidecar
First Edition

Practical Fox, Portland Oregon

© 2018
All rights reserved. First edition published 2018.
Cover image by Taxiro
Cover design by Carly Cohen
Editing and production by Practical Fox
Paperback ISBN: 978-0-9893658-8-8
eBook ISBN: 978-0-9893658-9-5
Library of Congress Control Number: 2018942715

For Robin Rhodes, who encouraged me to view cultural anthropology through a feminist lens.

1

In Which Professor Kelly Heads West

Professor Nell Kelly was thinking of two things as the Empire Builder rocked across the drab North Dakota plain: children (which she did not want) and the bones of the long dead (which she did want).

There were several intellectual reasons for not wanting children, and she'd given them to her mother every day and to her aunts at every family gathering. The most important, and the one she repeated most often, was that she wanted to attend a university and study the sciences, which hardly left time for tending to children. This usually stunned her aunts into silence, or they would laugh nervously, as if she'd spoken Japanese and they were embarrassed to admit they didn't know the language. Or they would say, "You can't be serious." Oh, she was serious. She had the research to back her up, and she would lay it out at the drop of a hat. She'd spent hours in the library in town looking up global

1

population figures. There were enough people in the world already. In 1913, the most recent year her library had in the stacks at the time, there were nearly two billion people on the earth. "With a B!" she would tell her interrogator. "You'll change your mind," her aunt would say with an infuriating wink. "You'll find a man at that college, and you'll want to settle down and have babies."

Now it was 1926. She had attended university—Barnard on scholarship, no less—and she hadn't changed her mind. In fact, she had revised the no-children speech with more up-to-date information—by 1920, the world population was nearly two billion—and she'd since given it to university boards of geriatric men in ties rather than middle-aged aunties in sun hats. She was now a professor of anthropology at that very same Barnard College in New York City, and she was inventing techniques for determining the age of human remains, not birthing babies.

The more immediate and emotional reasons for not wanting children were seated across the aisle from Nell. Two terrible brats were pinching and kicking each other on the less-than-sly while their mother read the *New Yorker*— two thousand miles from any of the events described in the magazine, Nell noted. The mother held the magazine folded back on itself in one hand and a smoldering cigarette in the other. The boy, who was being so studiously ignored by his mother, wore short pants and a newsboy cap; the girl was a couple of years older but still wore a fluffy frock and long braids. Nell had marched into a parlor and had her own braids clipped off the first week of her freshman year, in 1919. The parlor might as well have set up a chute and a pen, as her uncles did for sheep-shearing, so many girls were getting the chop as soon as they were out of their mother's houses.

Nell also had intellectual reasons for wanting the bones of the long dead. Nell was no necromancer. She had studied anthropology, chemistry, and geology at Barnard and created her own specialty in the dating of human remains. Her work was groundbreaking. Her work would change the discipline of archaeology as everyone knew it. And yet she could not attend, let alone teach, at Columbia University, where Franz Boas, Father of Modern Anthropology, was installed. It was across the street, for the love of Darwin.

She was on this slow boat of a train full of old people and young families because Dr. Harold Flagely of the University of Oregon had asked her to identify and date the remains of a human found in a rural part of the state. She had jumped at the opportunity. Here was a chance to prove that her new techniques were valid in the field. Columbia would have to notice. It was a very public case. Ever since those monkey trials the year before, archaeology and Darwinism were hot topics. Her own name had been in bold type in one of the New York rags; her mother had seen it and called her rooming house to express her dismay at Nell's reputation as a controversial intellectual. That, according to Nell's mother, was not the way to find a husband. Nell agreed.

The publicity would also help Dr. Flagely establish a proper anthropology department at the University of Oregon. He'd already roped in none other than Margaret Mead's ex-husband to bolster his cause on the cultural anthropology side; an important archaeological discovery incorporating the latest scientific techniques would clinch the deal.

Nell had hoped that thinking of old bones and new departments, plus the clackety rocking of the train, would shut out the whispered whines of the children across the aisle, but her hopes dissipated faster than the smoke of the mother's cigarettes. The train creaked around every bend no matter how slight, and the children had nothing else to do but irritate each other—and Nell. She wished, not for the first time since boarding at Grand Central Station two days ago, that she could have afforded to upgrade the ticket Barnard had furnished for her to a private car. Maybe with a fold-down bed and meal service. But she was a farmer's daughter on a university per diem, so she rode coach with its worn-out upholstery and much-trodden carpet.

Up ahead, the bright summer sunshine was finally fading to purple over the mountains' majesty. Nell would never wish upon the first star of the evening, but she did take note of Venus sparkling in the twilight. Just because it couldn't grant wishes—like for the two children across the aisle to fall into sudden and irreversible comas—didn't mean it wasn't lovely. Nell unclenched her jaw and ran a hand through her strawberry-blond curls. She waited for a moment of relative calm on the tracks and then stood to make her way to the dining car.

She stood with her feet hip-width apart in the aisle to get her balance and bearings before walking down toward the doors at the end of the car. She was four cars back from the dining car, including the observation car, and she'd gotten quite good at walking without looking like a fool. It helped that she had sturdy legs and a strong sense of balance; it also helped that she preferred low-heeled, laced shoes to fashionable T-strap numbers with delicate heels. Nell was sure the mother across the aisle with her cosmopolitan reading taste and her swirling cigarette smoke did not approve of Nell's plainly practical traveling suit and shoes. Though she was a thoroughly New Woman, there was nothing of the lithe flapper about Nell. Never had been, never would be.

She walked smoothly if not gracefully to the dining car while the conductor and his staff lit lamps in the darkening cars as the sun sank behind the Rockies. The concierge led her to the last empty table in the dining car, just inside the door, which had only two chairs rather than the regular four. One side of the table was pressed against the wall of the car; she took the seat facing backward. She never got motion sick, though she knew many people did. While she waited to see if she would get to dine alone, she watched the plains become foothills in the twilight. Everyone who came to dinner was seated at every available seat until the car was full. If one more person came to dinner, they would be Nell's dining companion.

The foothills of the Rocky Mountains were turning purple under the deepening blue sky when he entered, a lanky but not tall young man with freckles and blue eyes that sparked like a crackling Tesla coil. He wore a straw cowboy hat on his head and a plaid shirt with dungarees held up by a very large silver belt buckle. Nell wondered that the weight of the buckle didn't work against the purpose of the belt. The concierge gestured for the man to take the chair across from Nell, which he did. He removed his hat as he sat down and presumably hung it on a bony knee beneath the white tablecloth. He was as ginger as Nell's old tomcat back on the farm. Everything about this scrawny redheaded cowboy seemed unattractive on paper, but Nell found him intriguing.

"Casey McCormick," said the young man as he thrust a hand across the table.

"Nell Kelly," Nell returned with a firm shake of his hand. She was impressed that he shook her hand in a normal, friendly manner rather than holding her hand limply and delicately, as if she were made of porcelain, the way so many New York young men did. Nell and Casey dropped their hands to their laps and ordered Cokes from the server who had appeared tableside.

"What's a pretty young girl like you doing traveling alone?" Casey asked. It was the first question almost everyone had asked her in the past two and a half days, though no one else had called her pretty.

Nell gave her standard reply: "I'm an anthropologist on my way to the University of Oregon on behalf of Barnard College." It usually stopped the uninteresting and intrigued the interesting, cutting out the dreaded small talk either way.

"Wow, Barnard. One of the Seven Sisters, yeah?"

Nell could not help but curl her lip at what she considered a diminution, and the cowboy could not help but notice.

"How long you been on this train?" he tried instead.

"Actually, I've been on two trains. I switched in Chicago two days ago. Three days of travel total. We'll be in Portland in the morning." She snapped her napkin to unfold it and placed it on her lap as the server brought their drinks. Nell ordered a bowl of buttered noodles; Casey ordered a steak with mashed potatoes. He drank an inch of Coke from his curved glass then lowered the glass beneath the linen-covered tabletop. He glanced down the car then pulled a flask from his hip. He refilled the glass to the very brim then raised an eyebrow at Nell.

She could plainly smell the esters wafting from the whiskey. "No, thank you," Nell said.

"You dry?" He glanced at the waiter delivering drinks to another table and seemed a touch worried.

"No. But I need to be at my best in the morning."

Casey relaxed and took a sip. "You got a cabin?"

"No, a seat in coach." She stiffened.

He shook the flask under the table, sloshing the whiskey against its metal sides. "Sounds like you could use a sleep aid."

She smiled. "No, thank you."

"Ask if you change your mind." He tucked the flask in a hip pocket. "What you heading to Oregon for?"

"Professor Harold Flagely invited me out to the University of Oregon to test my new ideas incorporating geology and chemistry into the process of determining the age of human remains." If that didn't stop him, nothing would.

"That is a mouthful," Casey said. "It sounds like important scientific work. I can see why you're staying sober." He sipped his spiked Coke and tipped his chair away from the table until the curved wooden back of it touched the wall behind him. "Flagely," he said. He looked up in thought and pursed his lips. Then he tipped his chair forward and came halfway across the table in his excitement. "Gunn Flagely! You know her?"

Casey took three steps down the ladder of Nell's opinion of him. "I do not know her, but like everyone else, I know *of* her. She is Dr. Flagely's daughter. I will not be working with her."

Casey whistled low and shook his head. "She's a real firecracker, that Gunn Flagely."

"So I hear," Nell said. "Do you read her books?" Nell heard the cold, accusatory tone of her voice and decided she didn't care.

"Naw," Casey said, tipping his chair back again. "I hear stories like everybody else. I'll leave the actual reading of Miss Flagely's books to others. I don't have time, to tell the truth. Those that do read 'em seem to like telling everyone else what's in them anyway, so I feel like I'm enough in the know."

"Indeed they do." Casey climbed back up two rungs on Nell's opinion ladder. The server brought their dinners and placed them with a little flourish on the white cotton tablecloth, and the two travelers tucked in. The noodles were blandly buttery and barely above room temperature. Another diner might have complained, but she ate to fuel her brain and body for the task at hand, not for pleasure.

Nell hated small talk, but she wanted to get ahead of any talk of Gunn Flagely. So she gave it a shot. "How long have you been on this train?"

"Oh, I just got on in Glasgow, a couple stops ago. One quick overnight in one of those upright coach chairs for me, then a long ride in an old truck to my uncle's ranch in eastern Oregon. I'll be there by dinnertime tomorrow. The steaks will be a sight more fresh than this old guy." He stabbed his fork into the hunk of gray meat on his plate and held it up for Nell's inspection. "But what are they gonna do on a train? I'm happy they feed me at all." He put the steak down, cut a piece off, and forked it into his mouth.

"Dr. Flagely is to meet me in Portland at his home, then we'll drive down to the University of Oregon in Eustace the next day."

"Eugene," Casey said between bites.

"Eugene, yes. Thank you. That's where the archaeology department is, or will be if all goes well this summer, and where I'll set up a state-of-the-art lab for identifying what may be the oldest human remains ever found in North America." Nell twirled too many slippery lukewarm noodles around her fork, but she ate the huge bite anyway. She had been told once by a beau that her table manners were a unique delight.

Casey chewed his way through his overcooked steak and mashed potatoes. He used the last small pieces of fatty steak to sweep up the remains of the mashed potatoes. He leaned back in his chair again and took in Nell.

"Human remains, huh? You study old bones?"

"I do," Nell said.

"Not many women doing that, I bet. Not many people at all doing that, come to think of it."

"It's true. There aren't many people in the field at all, and especially not women, but I find the story of mankind's evolution fascinating. So many questions to answer! The missing link is still missing, you know. I'm working to make the answers more precise and fill in those blanks in our evolution." She waited for the angry tirade, the pity at her path to Hell, or the tight-lipped reference to monkeys. She got none of these from Casey.

"Seems like important work, especially these days," Casey said nodding. "This is a big deal, right? You've been summoned from across the country." He waved his arm grandly and set his chair aright.

"Invited, not summoned," Nell said with a smile.

"Either way, this Dr. Flagely wants your expertise. I bet you'll be aces." He finished his Coke and set the glass on the table, then he fished a few dollars out of his wallet. Nell reached for her purse, but Casey said, "I've got this one, Professor Kelly."

"Thank you, Casey Cowboy."

"Can I interest you in a more relaxing Coke in the observation car?" He stood and tapped a short, ragged fingernail on the flask in his pocket. "I think you'll find I'm conversant in subjects beyond cattle."

Nell wanted to say yes to the spark-eyed cowboy with the whiskey in his pocket. But what she said was, "I should get back to my seat and rest up for tomorrow. I appreciate the offer. And while it's nice of you to pay for my dinner, it's really unnecessary. I have my own money."

"I'm sure you do. And so do I, and mine's already on the table. Done deal."

Nell stood and offered her hand, so Casey again shook it firmly.

"We can at least walk to the observation car together," Casey said. "It might seem awkward for us to say good night and then follow one another along the only route through the train."

"Excellent point," Nell said. He moved aside and allowed her to pass through the door. The very next car, Nell now remembered, was the observation car.

Casey stopped behind her at an empty seat. "There are two free seats, Professor." He stood waiting with a grin. "We can watch the Rockies fly by as we head for Spokane."

"It's getting dark."

"Stars to see," he tried. "Astronomy."

"Not my strong suit," said Nell.

"Suit yourself. Good luck with those old bones, Professor Kelly," Casey said as Nell backed away along the aisle.

"And good luck with your cows, Casey Cowboy."

He waved and sat in the chair. He did a quick check around the observation car before taking his flask from his pocket. Nell turned and opened the door between cars. She hoped against hope that the kids in her car were asleep or, even better, gone.

2

In Which Nell Kelly Kicks Herself a Couple of Times

The kids had indeed been asleep, and the train's creaking had quieted down once it was over the Rockies. She hadn't even noticed when they'd stopped to decouple the train at midnight in Spokane. She only woke when the sun streamed along the Columbia Gorge and the train was a couple hours outside Portland. She ate the last hard breakfast biscuit that she'd packed in her New York apartment, but her little wax-paper-wrapped butter supply was long gone. *This is how the pioneers must have felt as they approached Oregon,* she thought as she swallowed the dry biscuit along with sips from a paper cup of water. The family across the aisle had silently disembarked while Nell slept, leaving her a pleasant morning to prepare for her arrival in Portland and her meeting with Dr. Flagely.

She took a folded piece of stationery from her handbag and carefully opened it so as not to tear it along the worn-out folds. *Dear Nell Kelly,* it began:

> I am delighted you have accepted my invitation to teach my students and myself your innovative, cross-disciplinary methods for determining the age of human remains. The subject of your methods in Oregon may, if you are able to prove it, be the oldest human remains ever found in North America. It may set our ideas about *Homo sapiens sapiens'* occupation of this continent on fire. I admit, I do hope it will.
>
> When you arrive in Portland on June 16, please take the Belmont streetcar from downtown Portland to 34th and Belmont. As you have spent several years attending and teaching at Barnard College in New York City, I trust you'll find our simple, aboveground public transportation system straightforward. I will meet you there and walk you and your belongings the one block to Mohle House, my permanent residence.
>
> We'll depart for Eugene and the University of Oregon the next morning, after you've recovered from your cross-country journey. We have all summer to spend in the lab; you'll be grateful, I think, for a day in the sunshine before we begin.
>
> In anticipation of your arrival,
> Dr. Harold Flagely

Nell could recite the contents of this letter more readily than she could the Gettysburg Address or any verse from the Bible, but she still double- and triple-checked the instructions: *Belmont streetcar to 34th and Belmont. I'll meet you there.* Nell Kelly had been called many things—standoffish, off-putting, too smart for her own good—but not once had she been called unprepared.

She folded the paper and tucked it away. She had seen grainy photographs of Dr. Flagely in scientific journals, but would that be good enough? Were a white mustache and glasses enough to recognize a man on a street corner in Portland, Oregon? She imagined their meeting: he would ask, "Nell Kelly?" and she would turn to find a tall, skinny man with erect posture and a smile beneath his mustache.

"I am Professor Kelly," she'd say with a smile and an outthrust hand.

No, too formal, she admonished herself.

"Dr. Harold Flagely, I presume?"

Oh my god, no. This is Oregon, not the headwaters of the Nile.

"Yes," she imagined saying in a pleasant, modulated voice, neither too strident nor too soft. "And you must be Dr. Flagely." Then she would hold out her hand, which he would shake briefly in the most collegial manner, and the two of them would walk the one block to Mohle House.

The conductor came along the aisle to announce that the train's final stop would be at Portland's Union Station in about one hour, so this was the last call for coffee in the snack shop below the observation car. The sun bounced around on the small waves in the Columbia River and lit the dry, rounded hills of southern Oregon across the water. Nell rose from her seat with a full stretch, her fingertips nearly grazing the ceiling of the aisle, and walked through three cars to the observation car. Casey, Nell noticed with disappointment but not surprise, was not in the observation car.

Though he'd had a flask of whiskey with him, it was hardly enough to send a man into a drunken stupor, especially a cowboy. He must have returned to his seat elsewhere on the train rather than passing out for the night in the public car.

She could have stayed for even a few minutes to chat with him last night. What would have been the harm? She sighed and shook her head. She was always so focused on her thoughts that she often missed the butterfly on the tip of her nose, as her father always said. But ignoring butterflies had gotten her a master's degree from Barnard College, and distractions like butterflies and cowboys wouldn't get her into Columbia. Entomology was not her cup of tea in any case, unless there were insect artifacts found with human remains. That would be interesting. Maybe she should do a survey on insects as burial goods, or the types of insects likely to feast on ancient remains. She was following this train of thought when she nearly pitched down the steep staircase to the lower level. She grabbed at the railing as her foot came down hard on the step then carefully stepped down to order a paper cup of black coffee. She carefully climbed the stairs back to the observation car and only then noticed the snowcapped, pointed mountain looming over the landscape to the south. *Never mind the butterfly on the tip of my nose,* she thought. *I almost missed Mount Hood.* She headed back to her seat for the final push into Portland.

It was for the best that she'd come straight back to her car after dinner, she decided as she sipped the lukewarm coffee. She felt rested, if not refreshed, after three days on a train with limited washroom opportunities. She had read the latest of Boaz's monographs on native tribes of the inland Northwest, and she'd had time to plan her first encounter with Dr. Flagely. Things were going to be just swell.

The train crawled along between another river and a forested hillside then slowed to a stop at Union Station. Nell stepped out into a surprisingly warm morning. The train cars had carried the cool air from the mountains through the gorge, so she hadn't realized that it was setting up to be a scorcher. This wasn't going to do her navy-blue jersey traveling suit any favors. She gamely found the porter who had loaded her small trunk and large bag onto a cart. She set off for the front doors of the station with the porter and her bags on her heels.

Before she reached the brass-framed glass doors, a hand gripped her elbow. She turned on her heel, ready to swing. She'd had three older brothers, after all. She checked herself before clocking the grinning freckled face of Casey Cowboy with her fist.

"Good morning, Professor Kelly," he said, releasing her elbow.

"Good morning," Nell said, unclenching her fist. The porter slowed the cart to a stop beside them.

"You ready for your big day?" Casey tucked his thumbs into the belt loops of his dungarees.

"I am, thank you. I did need to get back to my seat last night to plan for today."

"I hope you find Oregon to your liking."

"Oh, I'm sure it'll be fine, though it hardly matters. I'll be spending my summer holed up in the lab with a bunch of equipment and very old bones."

"Try to get out some, okay? Fresh air is good for you."

Nell was touched that he seemed concerned rather than

prescriptive, like most people who couldn't fathom the idea
of a woman in a laboratory. "You'll get enough fresh air for
both of us this summer, riding the fences and roping steers,
or whatever cowboys do on your uncle's ranch."

"Branding. Don't forget branding."

Nell held Casey's gaze, which became quizzical as he
waited for her to pick up the conversational ball. When
she didn't, he looked toward the cars and carts arriving at
the station entrance. "Well," he said.

"Yes, I've kept the porter waiting long enough."

"And Dr. Flagely."

"Yes! And Dr. Flagely." She held out her hand. "Thank
you for dinner last night, not that you had much of a choice
for dinner companions. Have a nice summer."

"You too." Casey shook her hand and let her go.

Nell started again toward the doors with the porter at
her heels. He found her a cab to take her to the streetcar
line, and she tipped him as generously as she could afford.
Another per diem would be sent from the college to the
University of Oregon, so she had to make the couple dollars she had left last one more day.

Luckily the cab ride was short and the streetcar was
cheap. A bearded man in cork-soled boots and a shirt that
looked as if it had been recently washed and was still in
need of a wash at the same time hoisted Nell's trunk into
the streetcar's vestibule. Nell turned to thank him after
paying the conductor, but the bearded man hadn't hopped
on board himself. He was already half a block away, saun-
tering along with his hands in his pockets.

She took a seat where she could see her trunk and watched
what passed for a city roll by her smudged and dusty window.

The buildings were low by New York standards, even downtown, with none reaching above a half dozen stories or so. The blocks were short, with an intersection coming every few feet it seemed. The waterfront was crowded with businesses using the Willamette River as a trade route. As the streetcar crossed the Morrison Bridge, she turned back to see men and boats buzzing along the shoreline. The car crested the slight slope of the bridge, and she could see more of the same commerce along the eastern bank of the river. But quite quickly, as they passed the industrial center along the water, the neighborhood filled with brick apartments and wooden houses with wide front porches. A few people sat on these porches fanning themselves in the midday heat. She'd been expecting the notorious Northwest rain and gloom, with the mud and misery that came with it. This bright, dry sunshine and a hot breeze rustling through the trees that lined Belmont were not at all what she'd imagined. She hoped the dresses she'd packed would still be comfortable. She really hoped the lab she'd be working in had electric fans.

The streets conveniently counted up from First at the water's edge to, well, infinity as far as Nell knew. She only needed to concern herself with Thirty-Fourth Avenue, which is where she got off, dragging her trunk to the curb behind her. The intersection was a busy one, with restaurants and small stores along both sides of the street. There were plenty of people about, so Nell put on the expression she'd practiced on the train: pleasant professional woman looking for someone in the crowd. People smiled and nodded at her or wished her a good afternoon, but no one said, "Nell Kelly?"

No one.

It was hard to keep up this expression. The slight smile on her lips started to make her cheeks hurt, and her calves were aching from subtly standing tiptoe to see above the crowd for an approaching gentleman of a certain height and age. Nell was not a tall figure; she sometimes resorted to hiding a crate behind the lectern when lecturing in large rooms.

After fifteen minutes, no one came to shake her hand and walk her to Mohle House.

She moved her trunk under the awning of a restaurant on the corner and sat down on it. She decided on a new expression: patient woman waiting. She crossed her ankles and arranged her hands in her lap, then set her spine in an erect posture and went for what she hoped was a placid look on her face.

Twenty more minutes went by. No one came.

Nell felt her placid expression becoming peeved as she calculated the miles she'd traveled to meet this man. Her posture suffered under every drip of hot perspiration that rolled down her back. She knew no one else in this sweat-filled, dusty Hades—actually, she knew no one at all. She'd never met Dr. Flagely. She took the worn-out letter from her pocketbook and read it again: *34th and Belmont.* She checked the street signs: *34th and Belmont.* All she knew was this corner.

She did know one more thing, she realized: Mohle House. It was only a block away, according to the letter. This brightened her prospects, until she realized she had no idea in which direction Mohle House might be. She could barely carry her trunk herself—her farm-built muscles having atrophied to a more socially acceptable feminine weakness during her years at Barnard—let alone lug it up and down each of the cardinal directions in search of a house she'd never seen.

She looked left and right. Belmont Street was entirely commercial for the next few blocks east and west. That eliminated two directions. She stood and repasted the pleasant expression on her face then asked of the next woman who passed, "Excuse me, but could you possibly tell me where Mohle House is?"

The woman's eyebrows shot up as she took in Nell from frizzy copper-blond head to low-heeled shoes. "You don't seem the type," she said, "but it's just up there, that dark-red house. *Everybody* knows where Mohle House is." She walked off looking far more amused than Nell felt the woman should.

What did she mean by Nell not seeming the type? She had been studying archaeology and human remains for years; surely that time had left an imprint of intelligence and capability upon her. Surely she was the type to meet Dr. Flagely and visit him at Mohle House. She was Professor Nell Kelly of Barnard College. She was indeed the type.

The nerve of that woman electrified Nell's own nerve. She stopped the next likely young man she saw and said, "I'm sorry, but my escort was unable to meet me at the streetcar stop. Would you be able to help me carry my trunk to Mohle House? I can pay you a little. It's only a block away."

"Oh, I know where it is," said the young man. His blond hair glistened with sweaty pomade. "I'd be happy to help." He lifted Nell's trunk by its handles and headed down

Thirty-Fourth Street to the north. Nell picked up her suit-case and strode along behind, glad to have found someone to help but a little worried by his knowing tone.

At the next intersection, a much quieter residential one, the young man turned up a sidewalk leading to the dark-red Victorian-era house with spindles on the railings and gingerbread at the gables. He carried her trunk up two sets of stairs to the porch. Nell followed, her bag banging against her shin with every step. At the top, she handed the man a quarter from her purse. "Thank you so much for your help. I couldn't have done it without you."

"Keep your money," he said with a wave of his hand. "Any friend of Flagely's is a friend of mine. And half of Portland. And, from what I hear, Manhattan. And probably Tim-buktu, too." He stuck his hands in his pockets and hopped down the stairs, whistling as he walked away.

Nell was surprised to find that a professor of anthropol-ogy was so popular in his neighborhood. She decided not to hold it against him—yet—that he had forgotten their appointment. She had her own dose of absent-minded professoritis, she knew. She also thought every encounter she'd had in Portland so far was a little strange. You don't spend years of your life in New York without being a little suspicious of the overly friendly, even if you are, as her colleagues called her, a lab rat. She watched the young man walk back to Belmont Street and turn the corner. She turned back to face the wooden door.

Nell peered through the holes in the lacy white curtain that shrouded the window, but she could see none of the dim interior. She pressed her palms along her suit jacket from ribs to hips in an attempt to unrumple herself in the heat. She swiped a fresh coat of paint on her lips and drew her shoulders back. She rapped her knuckles on the door.

No one came.

This was becoming maddening. Where was this Dr. Flagely? He had known what time the train would arrive, and it had even been on time, despite traveling thousands of barren, boring miles across the Dakotas. He said he would meet her at the corner, and he hadn't. He'd said she could stay at Mohle House, but there was no one answering the door. She had half a mind to turn right around and head back to Barnard, but the thought of another three days on a train without a bath or a replenishment of her funds was intolerable.

She set her jaw, rapped again more loudly, and willed Dr. Flagely to answer his door.

After a moment, she heard footsteps. Her shoulders unclenched.

Then she heard light, feminine laughter and the padding of bare feet on wood floors. She stopped breathing. *No*, she thought. *No, no, no, no.*

The door was flung open by a tall woman about Nell's age with a shining slick of black bob and bright red lipstick. She seemed to be wearing only a silk kimono. Behind her padded a barefoot lion of a young man, sun-brown from his curly locks to his navel, which Nell could plainly see, as a white sheet was wrapped around his waist and trailed behind him like the train of royal robes.

"Can I help you?" asked the woman.

This isn't possible, Nell thought. *I cannot have traveled three thousand miles for this. I cannot have been left standing and sweating on the corner for this. I cannot be standing on a front porch in Portland, Oregon, with…with…Gunn Flagely.*

3

In Which Nell Finds More Disappointment and Horror

Nell set her jaw and drew herself to her full height of five-foot-three, which even in her shoes did not put her at eye level with the willowy, kimono-wrapped Gunn Flagely, who stood in bare feet on the dark wood floor.

"I'm Professor Nell Kelly, of Barnard College, and close associate of Franz Boas of Columbia University. Dr. Flagely was to meet me today." The heat and her haughty anger flushed Nell's cheeks bright red.

Gunn took Nell in from top to bottom and back again. The leonine creature behind her held his gaze on Gunn. "You're a bit overdressed compared to Julian and I, but please do come in. Daddy was held up at the dig site. He said you'd be arriving today." She stepped back to allow Nell room to enter the foyer with her pocketbook and suitcase. "Julian, do be a dear and bring Professor Kelly's trunk in."

The man stepped forward to do Gunn's bidding. "You may

want to put trousers on first," Nell said to a photograph of a
young woman in Gibson-girl garb that hung on the wood-
paneled wall. It was far safer for Nell to look at the photo of
the woman, who had a strong resemblance to Gunn, than
at the man in the sheet. Though she was guilty of sneaking
a peek to see if he heeded her recommendation about pants.

He merely shrugged, wrapped the sheet more firmly
around his hips, tucked one end into the makeshift waistband, and brought her trunk inside. He looked at Gunn,
who instructed him to take it upstairs to the guest bedroom.
He squeezed between the two women, his bronze arm
brushing the small of Nell's back as she continued her in-
depth study of Gibson-era hairstyles, and climbed the stairs.

"Well, you're probably in need of refreshments. And
you're definitely in need of refreshing," Gunn said. Nell
bristled, and Gunn noticed. "I meant no offense, Professor. But you have been on a train from New York for days,
yes? That doesn't exactly leave a girl smelling like roses
and feeling like sunshine. I should know." She turned and
padded down the short hallway, obviously expecting Nell
to follow in her perfumed wake. Despite not wanting to
out of sheer contrariness, Nell did.

They walked through a doorway into another small hallway with another staircase. Gunn gestured to her left with
a sweep of her alabaster hand. "Here is the washroom." She
swept her right hand forward to another doorway. "There is
the kitchen. If you want to make a pit stop after your long
journey, I'll do my best to put together a luncheon in the
kitchen. But don't get your hopes up. My culinary technique
is not my claim to fame." She winked at Nell, who refused to
acknowledge knowing what claim Gunn Flagely had on fame.

"Thank you," Nell said with a curt nod. She did need refreshing.

She used the toilet, glad to see that indoor plumbing and flushing mechanisms had made it all the way out West. When she stood at the sink to wash her hands and maybe splash water on her face, she was appalled at what she found. Her hair was like strawberry-blond lambs' wool clumped at her neck, and her freckles looked like dirt splotched across her hot, pink face. Maybe it was dirt splotched across her face. Her eyes were bloodshot, and her lipstick was long gone. This was what Casey Cowboy had called pretty at dinner on the train? Maybe it was better that Dr. Flagely hadn't seen her in such a state. She sighed and ran her wrists under a cool stream of water. She wished Dr. Flagely had met her as she stepped off the streetcar. Now she had to contend with the porcelain perfection of the cultural anthropologist Gunn Flagely. The cultural anthropologist who studied the sexual practices of anyone she could convince to let her drop in and take notes. Nell gripped the sides of the sink and bowed her head. She took three deep breaths to lessen her frustration, then she relaxed her shoulders and her grip. She splashed cold water directly into her eyes in an attempt to constrict the blood vessels and look less haggard. Then she did the same all over her face. It would have to do until she could take a full bath. She used the brush that must have been Gunn's to unknot the mess on her head as best she could. Then she reapplied a swipe of pink on her lips and took another look. Much better. And cooler. She was hungry.

Nell exited the restroom and found Gunn in the kitchen. She was leaning on a square counter set in the center of the room with stools at either side. There was an electric fan in front of the screen door behind Gunn, its breeze blowing her kimono against her long, slim legs. She'd laid out bread, cheese, fruit, and meat on a cutting board.

"I hope this will do," Gunn said. "It's my favorite kind of cooking—the kind where you don't have to cook at all. Especially on these hot days."

Nell placed cheese on a small slice of bread and said, "I expected rain. That's what the Northwest is known for, right?"

"Not in the summer," Gunn said as she popped a piece of ham in her mouth. She chewed and swallowed before continuing. "Though summer came early this year. It's not normally this hot and dry until the Fourth of July."

Nell looked around the kitchen as she chewed. She was feeling much better now that she'd splashed the dust off her face and eaten something more than her last stale biscuit. There was a sink, an icebox, a stove and oven, but no clock. "What time is it? I've completely lost track."

Gunn pulled up a wide, embroidered sleeve to reveal a leather-strapped man's watch. Its face was nearly as wide as her wrist. "It's nearly two o'clock." She held the watch so Nell could see it better. "It's an aviator's chronometer. Amelia Earhart gave it to me. Don't you just love it?"

Of course she did, Nell thought with equal excitement and dismay that Gunn Flagely knew one of her own personal heroines well enough to receive a gift from her. "Is it too late to reach Dr. Flagely?"

"In Joseph? How did you want to reach him? Pony Express?"

"I imagine he's waiting for me there, if he's not waiting for me here." Nell looked around. "Don't you have a telephone?" She was getting more confused and unsure. Gunn was looking at her as if they were speaking different languages.

"Of course we have a telephone. It's Portland, not Vanuatu—or the New Hebrides, as the world insists on calling it. The dig site in Joseph is hundreds of miles away. Oregon isn't one of those adorable little East Coast states that you just want to tuck in your evening bag and take with you to a jazz club. It's big."

"Can we call him?"

"Have you been to a dig site?" Gunn asked.

"Of course."

"And was there a telephone in that dirt pit?"

"No."

"There isn't one at Daddy's dig site, either. He's got those grad students sleeping in tents and digging pits to piss in."

Nell didn't want to piss in a pit. She did not want to spend time with a woman who used the phrase "pits to piss in." She did not want to drive for days to find Joseph. She wanted Dr. Flagely to be waiting for her on the corner when she hopped off the streetcar so that they could drive to the University of Oregon, where a lab and a per diem check were waiting for her.

"Where is the University of Oregon? Eugene?" Nell asked as they finished up their luncheon platter.

"A couple hours south of here. That's where Daddy teaches." Gunn swept the crumbs from the board into the trash and rinsed it in the sink.

"Yes. That's where I'm to go. That's where the lab is, and the skull I'm to date."

"I thought I was kinky," Gunn said slyly, "but you're dating a skull?"

Nell looked at the tin tiles on the ceiling and took a deep, irritated breath before answering. "In conjunction with Columbia University, I've developed experimental cross-disciplinary procedures for testing archaeological remains to determine their ages more accurately." *In conjunction* meant all but sneaking onto the men's campus across Broadway with the encouragement of Franz Boas, father of anthropology and professor at Columbia. But it was, in Nell's mind, in conjunction.

"Whew! That was a hell of a sentence," said Julian as he walked through the doorway to the kitchen. He was dressed this time in a gray suit that did not obscure his leonine physique. It was the unruly, caramel-colored hair, Nell decided, that would always give him away as a beast rather than a man. He walked to Gunn and kissed her neck below the sharp ends of her bob.

"You should know from sentences," she said as he pulled away. "He's an English professor at Reed," she explained to Nell.

"And that's where I'm headed next. Last class of the afternoon, and then office hours. Thank you for a lovely lunch, Gunn." He waved and headed for the door.

"Anytime!" Gunn called after him. "You meet the nicest people on the streetcar," she said to no one in particular.

Gunn Flagely was not helping the cause of women's equality by sleeping with men she met on the streetcar, Nell thought. These flappers and jazz babies thought they were freeing women from drudgery, but they were just making it harder for the serious women of the world to be taken seriously. But that was neither here nor there. Or, more to the point, it was very much here, while Nell needed to be very much there—in Eugene.

"How can I get to Eugene this afternoon?" Nell asked as she drew herself a glass of crystal clear water from the faucet.

Gunn perked up from her post-Julian haze. "I'll take you!"

"That's very generous of you, but a train would be—"

"You've spent enough time and money on trains. I know you've been given a stipend by some university or other, but that doesn't translate to pockets loaded with coin. I doubt that trunk upstairs is a treasure chest. Besides, it's either that or work on my next book."

Nell looked into her water glass for an answer. There really wasn't an argument to be made. That she had even a few dollars left was thanks to Casey the cowboy's generosity in the dining car.

"That's what I thought. I'll drive you to Eugene. It's only a couple hours, and we can stay the night in Daddy's teaching cottage near campus while we figure out what to do with you. It's a bare-bones affair, that little house, and stacked to the roof with books, so you'll probably enjoy it. We can check in with Prof Martingale. He'll know what to do with you." She cocked her head and appraised Nell. "Probably."

Nell walked a tightrope between offense and relief. She was tired enough to go with relief, though she kept the offense in her back pocket for later. Surely it would come up again if she were going to spend an afternoon in a car with Gunn Flagely.

"You can drive?" Nell thought to ask. She herself could, having learned on the ancient Model T her family used to bump around in on the farm.

"I can better than drive," Gunn said as she slunk out of the kitchen. "Let me get my togs on, and we'll be off!" Nell heard Gunn's bare feet patter down the hall and up the stairs. She finished her water and washed out the glass.

She wandered into the next room, a dining room, where built-in cupboards and a sideboard displayed the collected trinkets and publications of Flagely *père et fille*. The marble top of the sideboard, which a more usual family would use as a buffet for serving, was backed by a mirror that reflected several naked figurines from a variety of cultures in various positions—some alone, some together, some sacred, some very, very profane. Above these figurines were built-in shelves with glass-paneled doors. These shelves showcased artifacts picked up by father and daughter on their anthropological adventures. At one end of the shelf, held upright by a purple-swirled, crystal-lined geode, were books and monographs published by one or the other Flagely, and in the case of a site where remains had been found with fertility figures, both Flagelys.

Gunn was about the same age as Nell herself, and she'd already published nearly a dozen monographs. How she found time to write while living such an infamous life on both coasts and on most continents, Nell could not imagine. The books she wrote were scandalous and salacious, appealing to the popular notion of anthropology as living among exotic, far-flung peoples, drinking native concoctions in Manhattan or Morocco, having sex, and whooping it up. Gunn Flagely's nonacademic books made no account of the data gathered, the taxonomies created, the cultural lineages determined. Gunn Flagely studied—if that was even the word—sex, whoever was having it and however they were doing it. Those books barely scratched the surface of a culture, and scientific understanding of human behavior never entered into the equation. Her books didn't even have equations.

Dr. Flagely's books, though, Nell had quite a bit of admiration for. He was kind of a rogue archaeologist without a formal anthropology department backing him, but he had to be. He had trained as a natural scientist, with a degree from one of the Ivies Back East. Archaeology as a science was new, and though Howard Carter and his exploits in Egypt had ignited the public's interest in ancient worlds decades before, it was a rough road getting those interested amateurs to follow along from glamorous gold-lined tombs to muddy old bones in the Pacific Northwest. But Dr. Flagely soldiered on, detailing and cataloging his findings as best he could and publishing monographs on his own dime through the University of Oregon's press. Nell had read every one.

Nell was still inspecting the spines of the books when Gunn clomped down the nearer staircase and arrived in the dining room. Gunn's hair was smooth as black silk, and her eyes were rimmed with kohl. Her lips were painted red to match her nails, and she wore a tweed riding suit, complete with man-style breeches tailored to fit her form and tucked into brown boots laced to the knee. All she was missing was the riding crop.

"Are we riding horses to Eugene?" Nell asked.

"Sure, about twenty of 'em," Gunn said as she strode to the side door at the foot of the stairs, leaving Nell to follow in her wake. She plucked two brown leather helmets and goggles from hooks on the wall, where they hung like gas masks from the Great War. "We're riding my Harley-Davidson." She tossed a helmet and goggles to Nell, who caught them reflexively.

"A motorcycle? But, my trunk," Nell said with a backward glance. "My things." *My very life,* she thought.

"They'll be safe here while we figure out what to do with you. Besides, you'll feel lighter without them," Gunn said. "Freer. Less encumbered." She raised her arms as if her soul were lifting along with the weight of Nell's trunk. Gunn opened the side door and strode out.

A garage was tucked under the dining room, and Gunn pulled the door open to reveal a drab green motorcycle with red pinstripes and a matching sidecar. She lifted the kickstand with her booted toe and pushed the rig out into the sunshine. Then she plucked a leather satchel from another hook on the garage wall and slung it over her shoulder. Nell eyed her own small purse and her tired traveling suit. Never had she felt so improperly dressed; she felt like an unfashionable egghead comparing herself to a brazen woman wearing trousers.

Gunn put the helmet on her head and buckled the strap under her chin, then put the goggles over her eyes and grinned. The goggles and the grin made the woman seem insane. Nell studied the motorcycle and sidecar again and wondered if she herself were insane for even thinking of getting in such a thing. The tires were skinny and wrapped around a wheel with dozens of spindly spokes. The engine was wedged into the frame right under the rider and exposed to the elements. The exhaust trailed along the right side of the beast, next to the metal sidecar, which had its own tiny, feeble wheels tucked under its bullet-shaped hull.

Gunn clapped her leather-gloved hand onto Nell's shoulder with a painful smack. "I know. She's beautiful." She strode to the bike, slung a long leg over the seat, and rested her hands on the grips. She kicked the engine to life, and a plume of smoke erupted from the tailpipe. Nell waved it out of her face as Gunn turned to call over her shoulder, "If you want to be a founding mother of archaeology, a bone-loving rival of my boner-loving friend Margaret Mead, you better climb in, sister."

Nell was too shocked by the whole thing to move. Gunn Flagely was more horrid in real life than she'd even imagined. But Nell could see no way around that sidecar. The little money she had left in her purse would barely buy a train ticket to Eugene, with none left over for food. If she didn't get to Eugene, she didn't get so much as a glimpse of that old skull, unless you counted the grainy photograph in the newspaper that would accompany the article about some other scientist verifying it as the oldest skull in North America. *Good-bye, tenured Barnard professorship. Farewell, possibility of being the first female instructor at Columbia University. Hello, marriage, kids, and a lifetime of needlework samplers: "I used to be a scientist" surrounded by stitched chickens and the goddamned alphabet.*

"Fine!" Nell said. She pulled her skirt in and climbed into the sidecar.

"Helmet and goggles, please," Gunn said. "Gotta protect that giant brain of yours, and we don't want your eyeballs popping out when this thing gets cranked up."

Nell did as she was told. She didn't see that she had a choice.

4

In Which Nell Kelly
Loses Her Head

Gunn piloted the Harley-Davidson through Portland's east-side neighborhoods, then opened the throttle all the way once she reached Highway 99, according to the signs Nell managed to read as they sped past. They passed flower farms where posies for picking waved in colored rows and fruit orchards where trees were heavy with sweet-smelling cherries and apricots waited to be harvested. They passed through Oregon City, which Nell knew from her grade-school days only as the end of the Oregon Trail, and Salem, one of the forty-eight state capitols she'd memorized. After about an hour—an eternity when measured from the inside of a hot, noisy sidecar—Nell was overtaken by a violent sneezing fit. Her eyes watered like Niagara Falls behind her goggles. A large painted sign at the roadside welcomed motorists to Linn County, Grass Seed Capital of the World. Tiny towns like Tangent, which lived up to its name, passed in a blur.

Three hours after hopping in the sidecar, Nell's nearly numb nether regions were in Eugene. Gunn navigated the tree-lined streets of the small city while Nell gawked at the apparent insanity of every citizen. They wore every color of the rainbow all at one time, on patchwork pants and dresses that seemed to have been handmade in an asylum. There seemed to be more bicycles than cars, even of the old-fashioned penny-farthing type, and people lazed in the city's shady green spaces as if a gangster had just emptied the clip of his Tommy gun while driving through town.

After a few minutes, Gunn rode her rig up onto the sidewalk in front of a large brick building on the University of Oregon campus. This being early in the summer term and late on a hot afternoon, there were few students rushing between classes. Gunn and Nell nearly had the campus to themselves. Gunn cut the engine, pushed up her goggles, and unstrapped her helmet from her chin to reveal her wide and amazingly, but not perfectly, still red smile.

Nell climbed out of her sidecar and spat like her brothers after a day of tilling on the tractor. She was not normally a spitter, but the situation and the road grime in her teeth seemed to call for it.

"That was the most miserable ride I have ever taken in my life!" She tore off her goggles and sweaty helmet and threw them onto the floor of the sidecar. "You call that tarmac? It's barely more than oily gravel. Insects assaulted my cheeks and flew into my mouth like little barn burners, the wind made my face feel as if it's covered in cobwebs, I'm freezing despite the heat, I will never look at grass or its seed kindly again, and I'm starving." She rubbed her knuckles in her itchy eye sockets.

"Don't rub your eyes," Gunn admonished, swinging a long leg over the rear tire to stand next to the bike. "You'll only give yourself puffy purple bags, and if you don't have the shoes to match, it is a ghastly look." Gunn leaned forward to repaint her lips in the motorcycle's mirror.

"How fast were we going, anyway? A hundred miles an hour?" Nell brushed her navy-blue traveling suit, which had seen far cleaner days, into place. This neatening up only revealed dark patches of sweat at her waist and on the small of her back. Lovely. Then she attempted to deal with her bob, which was both flattened against her skull by sweat and fluffed out and frizzy at the ends. She did not dare lean toward the motorcycle's mirror. Leather helmets were not Nell's friend, though Gunn's helmet didn't seem to ruffle her feathers any.

Gunn smacked her lips together and winked at her image in the mirror. "Half that," she answered. "A hundred miles an hour would jump the candlestick, though, wouldn't it? Those Indy cars can do it, but not just any old bucket of bolts on the street. Not even old Harley D here." She replaced her lipstick in her jacket pocket and hung her helmet and goggles on the handlebars.

"Where's Professor Martingale?" Nell asked.

"Right through there, Professor Impatient." Gunn gestured at a large wooden door. "Don't you want to freshen up first?"

Nell had no idea how she could be expected to do such a thing, having as she did one small purse, a nose full of pollen, and one of the earliest documented cases of motorcycle-induced helmet hair. "Dr. Martingale is a professor and a scientist, not a fashion illustrator. I'm sure the recovered

cranium and my imminent examinations of it are more
important than the state of my face or dress."

Gunn shrugged and flung the door open as if it were
made of paper. Nell caught it as she passed through and
was surprised when the heavy door shoved her into the
dim hallway like a scolding aunt. The frosted glass globes
hanging from the high ceiling in the hall weren't turned on;
the bright afternoon sun was shining through a window at
the opposite end of the hall and reflecting off the waxed
floor. Gunn and Nell walked half the length of the patterned linoleum floor, then Gunn turned sharply to her left
and rapped a little rhythmic tattoo on a door marked Dr.
Robin Martingale, Director, Life Sciences. It was, to Nell,
an impressive amount of gold leaf on the glass pane—an
amount she herself aspired to. She shared her office with
a constantly turning carousel of three associate professors, so her door had sliding nameplates that could be
easily changed.

A voice called out, "Come one, come all, to experience
the wonders of ethnobotany!"

Gunn pressed the door open and said, "I bet you say
that to all the girls."

"I do. And the boys too. Everyone can benefit from the
natives' knowledge of plants for work and play." Professor
Martingale hustled from behind his large desk, which
made the already small man seem elfin. He wore a suit
the color of wheat stubble in a harvested field—tan, bland,
and somehow scratchy even to look at. All three pieces—
jacket, vest, and trousers—were of the same material, with
a soft-looking white shirt underneath and scuffed brown
shoes of what looked like leather folded in a Chinese style

and held together by laces. Small, gold-rimmed glasses framed his eyes and a serene smile seemed to never leave his lips.

Dr. Martingale hugged Gunn, his fuzzy, pointed chin jutting up and over her bony tweed shoulder. Then he turned his bespectacled dark-brown eyes to Nell. "And who might you be, dusty lady? A friend of Gunn's?"

"Professor Nell Kelly, archaeologist," she said with her hand thrust forward. "Did you say 'ethnobotany'?"

"I did indeed, Nelly," he said with a slow, slow blink of his eyes that kept him from seeing Nell's annoyance at the diminutive nickname. "It's what I'm calling my work these days. Gunn's father is helping me with it. I'm a botanist by training, but I have found that the really interesting thing—the really, really interesting thing, right?—is the way people use plants. How they interact with them." He twisted his hands and forearms around each other as if they were vines. "It's all in how we use plants, right? For healing, for harming, for food, for structures. You put people and plants together, man, and abracadabra! The magic is right there. Take, for instance, my suit, which you seem to be admiring, Nelly."

Nell wished she were able to look away from the shapeless suit of an uncommitted color, which might be made of potato sacks, but she'd been trying to figure the wretched thing out for the past minute.

"I grew the hemp myself, retted it, combed it, spun it, and weaved the fabric on a loom I rented in a local cloth shop. I worked with a tailor to pattern the suit and then I sewed it myself, by hand." He extended his arms and admired his handiwork. "A year and a half from seed to suit. The same stuff we make rope for ships with, if you can believe it." Nell could.

Gunn crossed to a worn brown leather davenport and sat down, tucking one foot underneath her. Professor Martingale joined her on the davenport, leaving Nell obligated, though not invited by the professor, to take the deep-green leather wing chair opposite.

The professor looked at Nell and squinted. Nell thought his brain might work at a plant's pace. "Professor Nell Kelly, archaeologist," he said, putting her name and her purpose in his department together at last. He blinked slowly again, like a happy cat in a sunbeam, then exclaimed with wide little eyes, "Harold Flagely's skull!"

"Yes," Nell said. "It is getting late, and I would like to—"

"Right on, right on," said Professor Martingale as he stood again. "Harold told me to expect a real go-getter of a lady professor, a hard-headed scientist, if you don't mind my saying so."

"I don't mind at all," Nell said, rather pleased. She stood and followed him to the door.

The professor held it open for her. "Harold's office is the next door down. He's a professor of life sciences here for now while we work up a proper anthropology department. That's why you're here, yes? To give us a bit of a boost in the reputational department?" he asked over his shoulder as they walked.

"I certainly hope so, Professor," Nell said. Martingale hustled to catch up with her as she strode to the next door.

He unlocked the door to Dr. Flagely's office, which was nearly identical to his own but with a less lived-in look. The bookshelves weren't so well stocked, and the desk and chair stood nearly alone; only one armchair sat near the desk, presumably for a student on the verge of an academic breakdown.

"Harold's only been here two semesters, and not every day of those semesters. He's been driving across the state every chance he gets to look for more pieces of our friend here." He gestured at a cranium perched on a shelf.

"Is that it?" Nell whispered.

"It is," Martingale answered. "The hope of our department. Fame and felicity—though likely not fortune, this being academia—will come to the people and universities who pin down a date for that man's death—the earlier the better. Of course, those closed-minded monkey-trials people are hoping it's some drunk Indian who got lost, passed out, and died twenty years ago. Now that I mention it, the Nez Perce are keeping an eye on this cranium too. They hope it's one of theirs. Coyote, they call him. Trickster god. Creator of the People. They'd very much like to have their ancestor back. Have to talk to the folklorists about that one." Martingale blinked slowly.

Nell had crossed to the skull and picked it up gingerly. It was fragile and dirty, but nearly complete. Only a few chips and dings had befallen this fella since he had been buried. If he had been buried, rather than just dying alone and being left to rot. Dr. Flagely would know more about that. Whatever had happened had happened far longer ago than twenty years. She stared into its empty orbits. This was her ticket to tenure. There was no going back to the farm after a discovery like this, woman scientist or no.

"Any conclusions?" Gunn asked. She was leaning lacka-daisically on the doorframe with arms and ankles crossed.

To Nell, Gunn seemed ready to bolt as soon as the boring scholarly types released her.

"Of course not," Nell smiled, indulging Gunn's ignorance. "Studying this skull is my task for the summer. I've got new theoretical methods involving dendrochronology, and soil sample chemical analysis, and geological core samples, and likely more that may pin this man's death down to within a few hundred years. I plan on requisitioning a mass spectrometer, an X-ray machine, and a mountain of plaster of Paris. I don't suppose there's a proper lab in this building, Professor?"

"There are scientific labs in other buildings that may serve your purposes, unusual and intriguing as they are. They'll be closed now; it's nearing the dinner hour despite the glorious sunshine still all around us. Most of the remaining professors and students will undoubtedly have left for the afternoon. I can introduce you in the morning while we wait for Harold to return from easternmost Oregon." He clapped his hands and rubbed his palms together. "Having said that, I'd love a little predinner tea, something to work up the appetite. Gunn, care to join me?"

Gunn pushed off the doorframe and slipped her white hand into the professor's proffered elbow. "I'd love some tea."

"Is it all right if I stay here, Professor? I'd like to examine the skull further, if you don't mind. It's very exciting."

"Right on," said the professor. "When you're finished here, you'll be staying at Harold's cottage at the edge of campus. Gunn will show you to it later."

"Thank you," Nell said as the two strode off, Martingale taking two short-legged steps for every one of the long-legged Gunn's.

Nell placed the skull on the desk and sat in Dr. Flagely's chair to contemplate the skull and the enormousness of her task. The foundation of an entire department, not to mention her own tenure at the finest school of anthropology in the land, if not the world, depended on this skull being verifiably very, very old. She picked it up again and held it at eye level, as if it were Yorick. It was more complete than any cranium this old should be, and she could tell right off the bat that it was old. It was male, judging by the pronounced ridges of the temporal line along its sides. Its superciliary arch was also a bit more pronounced. It was lighter than the skull of a recently deceased male, but the bone had undoubtedly been eroded. Something about the skull set off an alarm for her. Was it the teeth? The jaw? Something seemed out of place for a skull so supposedly ancient and excavated in the Pacific Northwest.

A knock came on the open door, and Nell looked up. "Yes?"

A tall, thin man with silver stubble under the low brim of a black cowboy hat entered slowly. His heeled black boots tolled like wooden bells on the floor as he crossed to the desk where she sat.

"Can I help you?" Nell frowned and stood to meet the stranger. Professors wore the oddest clothing out West. At least it wasn't patchwork or hand-sewn hemp.

"I can help myself," said the man. "But I do appreciate your unlocking the door." He pulled a pistol from a black leather holster on his right hip and plucked the skull from her open palm. He held the gun between them, his elbow bent. He stood very close to Nell, and now she could see his nearly golden eyes gleaming under the shadow of his hat brim. He pinned her in place as much with his gaze as with his gun.

"Give Professor Kelly my regrets," he snarled. "He should know better than to leave such valuable things in the hands of little girls." He dropped the skull into a black felt bag and backed out of the room with the bag tucked under his left arm like a pigskin. His aim never wavered from Nell's midsection. He fixed her with one last hard look, which she returned, then he turned on a heel and walked on down the hall.

Nell recovered from her paralysis and ran to the door. "I'm Professor Kelly!" she yelled. She grasped the frame and leaned out, looking up and down the hall. He was nowhere, which was impossible, but she didn't have time to ponder impossibilities right now. There was a time for pondering and a time for action. Even Nell knew the difference. "Give me back my skull!" Her words echoed in the empty hall.

One door down, two heads with red eyes poked their heads into the hallway. A cloud of skunky smoke billowed out behind them. They turned their disembodied heads toward Nell. The bottom head, the one belonging to Martingale, said, "What's wrong?"

"The skull! It's gone! It was stolen!" Nell stood in front of the open door, keeping an eye on the office and both ends of the hall. Still no sign of the man in the black hat.

"Just now?" Gunn asked as she stepped into the hallway.

"Yes, a man in a black hat came in, pointed a pistol at me, took the skull, and took off."

It was a bit much for the plant-minded, slow-blinking Martingale to fathom, but Gunn was alert as a hunting dog. "Which way did he go?" she asked. She peered up and down the hall, her nose held high.

"I don't know. By the time I came to my senses and followed him, he had disappeared."

"Were you hurt?" Professor Martingale asked at last. He scrutinized Nell through red-rimmed eyes in search of blood or bruises.

"No, just insulted," Nell said. "He thought Professor Kelly was a man."

"No time for hurt feelings, Nell Kelly!" Gunn said. She stepped into the hallway and raised a pointed finger like a general leading a charge. "To the sidecar!"

Nell's shoulders dropped in dread.

"C'mon, Professor Kelly. You know what the guy looks like, and you want that skull like I want a stiff drink and a roll in the sheets."

Nell sighed and straightened her spine. It would have been so much easier if that evil man had just shot her. "To the sidecar," she said. Gunn cocked her elbows as if she were about to shuffle off to Buffalo and headed for the doors at an energetic clip, leaving Nell to hustle along behind.

5

In Which Nell and Gunn Find Clues

Gunn twisted her right wrist and flicked her left ankle. The Harley-Davidson leaped forward with a burbling roar and bounced off the sidewalk while Dr. Martingale waved good-bye from the front steps of the natural sciences building. Nell leaned forward, ready to endure hours in this sidecar if it meant picking up the trail of the stolen skull and the man in the black hat. A sore gluteus maximus, minimus, and medius plus a permanent ringing in her left ear were small prices to pay for unprecedented archaeological discovery and invention. The alternative was having her position at the university usurped by a man. Probably that kid Smyth who'd just been hired as an associate prof, with his stints at Harvard and Yale, schools she couldn't attend if she wanted to. *Smyth*. A young man from old money would trump a single woman from the farm no matter how innovative her inventions. This skeleton could be the key that unlocked her continued professorship of all North American history—a skeleton key that worked much better if it kept its cranium.

Nell's heart raced, but the bike did not. It puttered around the outskirts of the brick-built University of Oregon campus for five minutes then stopped in front of a small, white house with brick steps leading to a low front porch. It was far less grand than the Flagelys' gingerbread-styled Mohle House in Portland. The grass in the front yard was shaggy and crispy in the early summer heat, and the eight-foot rhododendrons at each corner of the house retained a few bright fuchsia blooms, though like everyone except Gunn Flagely, they'd lost their starch.

Gunn slid her goggles and helmet off and hung them on the handlebar. She strode toward the front door as she removed her wrist-length leather gloves. "I didn't think you liked the sidecar," she said to Nell over her shoulder.

"I don't."

"Then come along, birdsong." Gunn strode onto the front porch. She ran her fingers above the doorframe, found a key, and put it in the lock. She returned it to its less-than-secure hiding spot and looked back at Nell. "Are you making a little nest in your sidecar?"

"I thought we were going to find the man in the black hat," Nell said. She blinked and felt her long but frustratingly pale blond lashes graze the lenses of her goggles.

"Do you know who he is?" Gunn asked from the porch.

"No."

"Do you know where his secret hideout might be?"

"No. I don't even know if he has a secret hideout. He does have a black hat straight out of Central Casting."

"Hardly the significant identifier we need if we're going to track down the bad guy." Gunn turned and opened the door. "We don't have a clue," she entered the unlit interior of the house, leaving the door open behind her, "but we might be able to find one here."

Nell stood and fumbled out of the silly sidecar, removing the goggles and helmet as she went. Every time she disembarked from that contraption, she felt like a foal learning to walk while having to remove unwieldy headgear with its hooves. When she reached the porch, she could see Gunn standing inside at a rolltop desk. Stripes of afternoon sun came through the slat-shuttered windows on the right side of the room. Gunn didn't flinch an inch when the screen door slammed behind Nell as she came in; she merely continued sifting through stacks of papers.

Nell stood in the center of an Asian rug similar to the blue one at Mohle House—anthropologists certainly didn't miss an opportunity to shop the bazaars when they went abroad—this one red with flowers twining around the edges and vines knotted in the center. A gray velvet camelback chesterfield sat under the windows to her right, and a large iron radiator with peeling cream paint crouched cold and unused under the front windows. If anyone but a professor lived here, this would be the living room rather than yet another office.

"Is this Dr. Flagely's cottage?" Nell asked.

"Daddy stays here during the week when school is in session. This whole street is filled with professors, which is why it's nearly empty now. Only a few are dull enough to stay all summer." She gave Nell a pointed look.

"Are you insinuating that I'm dull?"

"I'm not insinuating," Gunn said. "Don't just stand there—look for clues."

"What clues?"

"If I knew, I would have marched straight to a clue, dropped it in my bag, and headed out to dinner and a beer stein full of bourbon. You spend all day digging in the dirt looking for signs of life, or death, or something. Now dig for clues."

"I'm more of a scientific analyst than a digger," Nell muttered, though she knew the distinction was wasted on the flapper Gunn Flagely. The doorway in front of Nell led to the white-tiled kitchen, but a doorway to the left led to a short hallway and a restroom. That seemed promising. She found a little library tucked in the back room.

"Daddy must have known the skull would be valued by someone besides a blond from Barnard," Gunn called. "Surely if old Skully can establish an archaeology department all on his own merits, he's got some serious juju rattling around where his brains used to be."

Nell wrinkled her nose, first at the cranium being given a nickname and second at the idea that it carried "juju." So very cultural anthropologist. "Money!" Nell cried. "The man in the black hat took the skull for the money. It would be worth a fortune on the antiquities market."

"Brilliant deduction, Professor Kelly!" Gunn cried in triumph.

The bookshelves lining the walls of the library made the small room even smaller by a foot on all sides. There was a window with a miniscule student's writing desk on spindly wooden legs tucked under its sill. The desk was only big enough for one piece of paper and one planted elbow. A corkscrew piano stool served as a writing chair.

This library was neat, probably because Dr. Flagely did most of his writing and grading in the front room at the big desk. Nell was glad Gunn had taken on the search through that mess. Unsorted sheaves and slips of paper piled on a desk gave Nell the heebie-jeebies. She only had to contend with a few scraps of paper in a lidless cardboard box on the little writing table. There were notes in different hands, likely Dr. Flagely's and his graduate students', referencing texts on the shelves related to Nez Perce, Coyote myths, and the geology of the Snake River Valley. This last one she plucked from the shelf and tucked under her arm.

There were also pictures of a dig site with a lot of very pleased people holding the skull she'd so recently held herself. There was one of a tall man with a neat, white beard and rimless eyeglasses holding the skull while a group of dirty young people crowded around him to fit into the frame. Nell figured it must be Dr. Flagely with his dig team, and given the happy smiles on everyone's unwashed faces, it must have been taken on the day they lifted Skully—great, now she was calling him that—out of the ground. There were close-ups of the skull with black-and-white measuring tapes for scale and wide-angle shots of the team working away with garden shovels and paintbrushes to unearth as much information as possible. Nell felt the fire of jealousy burn in her chest. She examined the few pictures of the skull on its own in an attempt to embed its every feature, every chip, every stain, in her brain. Then she slipped one of the pictures into her pocket. *For the investigation,* she told herself.

She stacked the remaining photos and notes like a deck of cards and tapped them to neaten up their edges. As she

placed them back in the box, with one of the wide-angle
dig site shots on top, she frowned. She lifted it up close to
her eyes and peered at a shadowy figure at the edge of the
frame, near a line of trees. He was too far away and too out
of focus for her to identify his features, but the tilt of his
shoulders and his large black hat gave him away.

Nell took the other group photos from the stack and
scrutinized each one. He wasn't in every photo, but he was
in several, always at the edge, always in shadow, and always
wearing that damned bad-guy hat. *He'd been casing the site!*
Nell flipped the images to check for dates—the pictures
had all been taken about a month before.

Nell ran to the front room with the pictures in her hand.
"He's here!"

"Where?" Gunn turned 180 degrees and bent her knees,
ready to fight or fly as the situation required.

"Not here—here!" Nell held out the photographs, and
Gunn took them. "He's the shadow at the edge of these
photographs. You can tell by his ridiculous hat and, if you're
an expert in the human skeleton as it has changed over mil-
lennia as well as in the individual, by the tilt of his shoulders
and his posture. He carries his right shoulder lower than
his left, likely due to an early minor deformation of the
spine that caused an imbalance as his bones matured. As
he grew to adulthood, the bones—"

"Hot Nelly Kelly! You're right!" Gunn looked up from
the photographs. "About the man in the black hat being
on site. You lost me after that."

"The dates are written on the backs of the images. They
were all taken about a month ago. He was casing the joint
and waiting to make his move."

"But there are so many people swarming around the dig site like bees in search of honey he never got his chance," Gunn said. "He must have overheard them talking about bringing it back here for Professor Kelly. Plucking Skully from the hands of one egghead professor sounds like a much easier heist than fighting off a bunch of graduate students armed with pickaxes and shovels. And it was. He just had to wait for you to arrive and unlock the door."

"You don't have to sound so admiring," Nell said as she took the photos back from Gunn and tucked them in her purse. "But you're probably right."

"We figured out what he did," Gunn said with a red fingernail tapping her pointed chin, "now we have to figure out what he's about to do."

6

In Which Nell Gets a Lager and the Lowdown

Nell was stretched out on the chesterfield, one foot on the opposite armrest, one foot on the floor, one arm flung over the sofa's tufted camelback, one wrist resting on her over-heated forehead. Gunn remained perched at the edge of her father's desk, her red nail tapping her lip as she thought. The room glowed orange with the setting sun.

"Well, this isn't getting us anywhere," Gunn declared. "Our brains need food." She grabbed Nell's arm and pulled her to standing.

"I don't know how you can even think of eating at a time like this," Nell said. She gave Gunn's tall, skinny frame a once-over. "Do you eat?"

"Of course I eat. I don't live on cigarettes and whiskey alone. Although…" She shook off the thought and linked her elbow with Nell's. "We need food, and I know just the place. You'll love it." Nell doubted this.

The two women walked across campus to a white house with a red porch and open windows. Nell could hear talking and the soft *tink* of forks against plates as they walked up the steps. The main room was dark and cool, despite every table having diners. Gunn nodded at the skinny man in an ankle-length white apron standing near the bar. He returned her nod, and his long, greasy hair swept against his jaw. Gunn threaded her way through the room and took a table on the screened-in back porch. It was warmer out here, and everyone had a cigarette lit. There wasn't enough of a breeze to clear out the haze that hung around them.

Gunn opened her gold cigarette case and took a rolled smoke then proffered the case to Nell. She shook her head, and her curls created eddies in the smoky air around her face. "No, thank you."

"You don't smoke?"

"I never picked up the habit."

Gunn exhaled a cloud of more smoke. "You should. It's delicious. And sophisticated."

"It smells."

"Like mystery and danger," Gunn said with a sly smile.

"Like a brush fire," Nell said.

"Surely you drink," Gunn said as the string-haired waiter approached.

"I do," Nell said.

"Hey there, I'm Jay, and I'll be helping you out this fine evening." The skinny man in the apron held a pad and pen poised for their orders.

"I'd like a," Nell peered at her fellow diners, who all seemed to have alcohol in front of them, despite Prohibition being in effect across the country. She continued in a whisper, "beer and—"

Jay held up a long-fingered hand and smiled. In his normal voice, he said, "We've got porter, stout, lager, and a seasonal kölsch."

"Beer will be fine."

"Those are all beers."

"Oh." Nell looked from Jay to Gunn to Jay.

"We'll both have ice-cold lagers," Gunn said. "And I'd like the Spinach Inquisition salad."

"Right on," Jay said, noting this on his pad.

"And I'll have the Remembrance of Things Pasta," Nell said.

"Right on," Jay said. "I'll bring those right out." He saluted and disappeared into the house.

"Isn't this town dry?" Nell asked.

Gunn put on a very serious face and nodded solemnly. "Yes, Professor Kelly, it is quite dry," she intoned. "Not a drop of alcohol here, or anywhere in the West. We are a pious and abstentious people, particularly the ladies." She took a long drag of her cigarette.

Nell didn't know how she was going to eat or drink anything around the knot of nerves that had already taken up residence in her stomach. She rubbed her temples and thought of young Smyth moving from his desk to hers in their shared office.

"Let me tell you, Nervous Nelly, why I brought you to this particular restaurant," Gunn said as she crushed her cigarette butt in the little tin tray.

"To suffocate me with tobacco smoke?"

"I brought you here because this is the cheapest boarding house in town. They'll take anybody."

"I am not *anybody*," Nell said as she straightened in her seat. "I am the foremost expert on…well, that hardly matters now, does it?" She crumpled her paper napkin in her fist. "I'll just find me a man and make some babies like everyone says I should." She used the crushed napkin to wipe up the spit that had landed on the table as she spoke.

"Oh, for the love of Boaz, will you cut it out? Man or no man, you've got a brain in your head, unlike our friend Skully. Use it. Here, Jay is bringing your beer."

Nell sat up when the beers were placed on the table. They were light gold and very cold. She drank it with relief, like her brothers after a day in the fields, rather than sipping it delicately. No reason to pretend at big-city sophistication anymore, she figured.

Gunn sipped hers, leaving a delicate imprint of red lipstick at the rim of the glass, and then continued. "When Jay brings our dinner, show him the pictures from the dig site. You've got them in your purse, right?"

Nell brightened. "The man in the black hat might have stayed here!" Gunn smiled. "But he's always in the shadows at the edge of the pictures. Jay won't know him from Adam if I show him the few pictures I've got."

Jay came through the fog of tobacco smoke with two plates that he set in front of them. Nell asked him to wait, and he said, "I am a waiter." He smiled and nodded slowly at his joke. Nell took the pictures out of her little purse and showed them to him. He flipped through them slowly then shook his head and handed the bunch back to Nell.

"Sorry, ladies. I can't tell if I've seen that guy before or not."

"It would have been just yesterday, or maybe even this morning," Nell said.

"Nope," Jay said with a shrug. He started to turn away, but Nell stopped him.

"Wait! I saw him up close and in person. I know exactly what he looks like," she said. "He's tall, with silvery stubble and a big, black hat, and he had a pistol on his hip."

Jay frowned in thought, as if he were on the verge of a useful memory.

"Golden eyes," Nell said. "If you saw those eyes, you'd remember him."

"I did!" Jay said with a snap of his fingers. "I remember those crazy eyes. Lots of guys wear big hats and carry guns, even in this laid-back town, but that guy was like a wolf dressed in man's clothing. I brought him his breakfast this morning. I tried to make conversation, asked him about his plans for the day and all, but he brushed me off. Said he was in town for one thing, and then he was headed out east. Had some business with a Professor Kelly, he said." Jay was nodding his head like an excited pigeon.

"Out east, or Back East?" Gunn asked shrewdly.

"Out east, for sure," Jay confirmed.

"With a Professor Kelly?" Nell asked in confusion.

"Yeah, totally. You know him?"

"I do," Nell said. She looked at Gunn, her eyes wide. Gunn returned the look, her smile beaming. Nell nodded. Gunn plunked a few dollars on the table and drained her beer.

"To the sidecar!" she shouted.

Nell looked longingly at her pasta. "Now I'm hungry," she said.

"Good point, Professor. Let's eat while we can, then," Gunn said. "Another beer please, Jay."

"Right on," Jay said. "Hey, you want me to ask around about that wolf in a hat?"

Nell shrugged. "More clues couldn't hurt." She plowed into her pasta, glad to be hungry at last.

Several minutes later, Jay brought Gunn's beer and another scrap of information: he had asked around inside, and the bartender had seen the man in the black hat tear off in a black car with a long hood just before dinner service began. The bartender only took note because the man was dressed like someone about to tie the hero's girlfriend to the train tracks in a picture show. He even had a bundle tucked under his arm like a football as he ran to the car, and then he took off with a loud roar of the engine. For looking like a bad guy out of a movie, he hadn't seemed too secretive, the bartender told Jay.

"A long hood means a big engine," Gunn said. "Why be secretive when you've got speed?"

Nell speared her pasta faster and drank her beer so quickly she got a headache from the cold. "We're going to need to be faster than he is," she said and then wiped her mouth with her napkin.

"Are you thinking what I'm thinking?" Gunn asked.

"Yes," Nell said. "*Now* it's to the sidecar! And hurry!"

7

In Which the Chase Commences!

Gunn and Nell flew into Dr. Flagely's cottage—two women on a mission. Gunn skidded through the doorway on the left, and Nell hurled herself at the desk in the front room. It was only then, after running back to the house hand in hand with Gunn and barreling through the front door, that she realized she had no idea what she was after. She knew she was after the skull, of course, but what was she after here in the cottage?

Gunn poked her head through the doorway. "Come on! Let's get you into some traveling togs."

Nell had to admit that her jersey suit wasn't exactly side-car material, and she'd already been wearing it for days. It was more tired than she was. She followed Gunn into a bedroom at the front of the little house. Gunn had laid out a pair of men's dungarees with a plain brown leather belt, a white jersey undershirt, and a brown belted leather jacket on the white bedspread. It wasn't quite what Nell had hoped for, given Gunn's stylish brown tweed riding suit. Gunn was still rooting in the closet, so Nell waited in case she found something better.

At last Gunn emerged with a leather satchel similar to her own clutched in her hands. "This will serve you far better than that teensy thing," she said with a glance at Nell's pocketbook. She threw the satchel on the bed next to the clothes. "Well, get dressed! We've got a man in a black hat to catch, and that getup is not going to fly in the sidecar."

"I know," Nell said as she looked again at the mannish clothing on the bed. As if being busty and broad-shouldered weren't bad enough, now she was going to have to wear *dungarees*.

"Look, it's Daddy's house, not mine. You're going to have to make do. It's not like we're going to see a soul as we drive in the dark across eastern Oregon. They only finished paving the road last year."

Nell stifled a sigh and set herself to the task. She was hardly a Vogue-worthy fashion plate anyway. And she had worn dungarees as an undergraduate at dig sites. They felt so strange. She took off her dress and kicked off her shoes, then turned her back to Gunn and peeled off her silk slip.

"Oh, that's lovely," Gunn said, picking up the slip. "You can bring that along for a nightgown." She stuffed it into the satchel.

Nell stepped into the dungarees and buckled the belt nearly at the last hole. She slipped on the jersey and surveyed herself in the mirror. The dungarees were baggy, but the jersey draped nicely over her torso—maybe too nicely. She blushed and put on the leather jacket. She buckled that belt to keep everything from flapping in the wind and again looked in the mirror. This time, she had to admit that she looked quite the female adventurer. She wiggled the toes of her bare feet.

"Very Amy Earhart," Gunn said and turned again to the closet while Nell transferred the contents of her pocketbook to the satchel. It didn't take long: lipstick, coin purse, small wallet, small notebook, pencil. She thought about the book on Snake River geology, then figured it would do her more good when she returned than in the sidecar.

Gunn turned back around with black socks and brown brogues in her hands. "They're the best I can do." She shrugged.

Nell could hardly be picky, and the shoes looked sturdy. Would Boaz's darling Margaret Mead balk at men's shoes in the service of greater adventure? She would not. Nell took the shoes and sat on the bed to put them on.

The women took one final look in the mirror: the willowy tweed-clad flapper and the curvy leather-clad scientist. Nell had to admit she felt unstoppable.

"We've got a skull to save," she said.

"And not one more second to lose," Gunn replied.

They ran outside to the olive-green Harley-Davidson, barely stopping to lock the cottage door. Gunn straddled the leather seat and settled her helmet and goggles on her sleek head while Nell hopped more gracefully than before into the sidecar and crammed the leather bucket and goggles onto her frizzy head. The procedure was a lot easier in dungarees, and it helped immensely that it wouldn't matter how professional she looked at the other end of the ride as long as she had the missing skull in her hand.

Gunn twisted her right wrist, and they were off into the early night, the stars just beginning to twinkle behind the butte on the east side of town. Nell was surprised to find that there was a town tucked on the other side of the hill. It didn't seem to belong to Eugene as a disconnected little neighborhood; it had its own grocer and gas station. The little cluster of houses seemed to huddle together as if they were hiding in the butte's shadow, hoping big, bad Eugene wouldn't notice anyone was living only a mile or two outside town. They passed a small sign that whispered Glenwood, without any "Welcome to" or population number or town motto. Nell guessed, as they rode out of Glenwood a moment after entering it, that the unofficial town motto might be, "Please don't notice us."

Hardly had they left the little town, though, when they crossed the Willamette River into Springfield, which seemed to assert its independence beginning right at the city's boundary line. Springfield went to such pains to be distinct from Eugene and to not need its nearly twin city across the river that Nell assumed Springfield must need Eugene, with its university and county offices and such, quite badly. Springfield had its streetlights blazing in the purple post-dusk of summer, though there were few other people about.

The motorcycle began to sputter then, and Nell looked up at Gunn in alarm. Gunn's red lips were snarling below her goggles as she twisted the throttle and kicked at the clutch, but it was futile. The Harley burbled and choked and rolled to the curb while Gunn cursed it and its mother from here to kingdom come. "You don't even have a mother, you son of a whoring Wisconsin mechanic!" she yelled as she dismounted from the dead steed. She gave the back tire a swift kick then stalked along the sidewalk from streetlight to streetlight.

Nell pulled herself up to sit on the rim of the sidecar. "What's wrong? Is it broken?"

"It's worse than broken," Gunn said.

"What'll we do?" Nell said in a new wave of panic. "I used to help out with the tractors on the farm, maybe we can—"

"It's nothing you can fix," Gunn spat.

"You don't know what I can fix," Nell retorted.

"You can't fix stupid."

"Now, wait a minute. I didn't buy my way into university like some people—"

"Not you, Careful Nell Kelly. Me. I forgot to put gas in the tank." Gunn stopped pacing long enough to slap the metal teardrop tank with her leather-gloved hand.

"Oh."

"Service stations won't open until morning. That bastard in the black hat will be halfway across Oregon by then."

Gunn stood on the sidewalk and stared at the stars in the night sky made faint by the electric streetlights. Nell perched on the back of the sidecar with her feet on the seat and her hands clasped between her knees. At the same moment, the women both decided that there was nothing else for it but to do what needed to be done. Gunn took the left handlebar and Nell took the right, and they turned the bike back toward Eugene and Dr. Flagely's cottage.

8

In Which the Chase Is On

The few miles either woman could have walked in less than an hour took an hour and a half, thanks to the effort required to push a three-hundred-pound motorcycle three miles in the dark. There were few cars traveling between Eugene and Springfield at night, which was fine with Gunn and Nell. Every passing motorist was a potential murderer via vehicle, as the drivers didn't expect two women to be pushing a motorcycle along the road in the dark. And each pair of headlights robbed them of their night vision, no matter how quickly they looked away.

They crashed into their beds at Dr. Flagely's cottage, Nell downstairs and Gunn upstairs, without changing clothes or even taking off their shoes. Not even Nell, whose professional life was hanging by a black thread, could keep her eyes open long enough to worry much about it.

When she awoke, she stumbled into the kitchen, where a pert and perky Gunn Flagely was waiting at the kitchen table dressed in her tweed riding suit. She held a steaming coffee cup in her hand, a red half-moon of lipstick at its rim.

"Welcome to the world of the living," Gunn said. "There's not much for breakfast. I found some Quaker Quick Oats, maple syrup, and dried apples. That and a tea kettle was the best I could do."

"How long have you been up?" Nell asked as she lit the burner under the tea kettle with a match and scrounged in the cupboards for a bowl.

"Since the sun came up," Gunn answered.

Nell found a bowl on a nearly empty shelf; Gunn had used the other of the professor's two bowls. She took the only other coffee cup from the cupboard and filled it from the percolator on the burner next to the kettle.

"Did I miss the alarm?"

"No alarm," Gunn said. "I just tell myself as I'm falling asleep what time I want to be up."

"That works?" Nell looked at the motorcycle-riding, tweed-suit-wearing, kohl-eyed jazz baby who hadn't met a rule she liked in her life, not even her own. "Sunrise doesn't strike me as the time you want to be up."

"It can be. It really doesn't matter when I got to bed, or when I get up, or what state of wreckage I'm in in either case, as long as I get some sleep at some point." She raised her cup in salute. "Oregon-brewed coffee every time, I'm telling you. Strong stuff. Puts hair on your chest."

"I've been thinking about the man in the black hat," Nell said. She poured hot water on the oats and apples and sat at the small round table with Gunn.

"Do tell," said Gunn.

"He wasn't a scientist, that was clear. He had no idea who I was, and within my circles, I'm a known entity. There aren't that many cross-discipline female archaeology professors in the world. He merely dropped this artifact into a soft bag—small favors—and walked out. I think he'd been sent to collect the skull for someone else."

"An excellent hypothesis, Professor Kelly."

"But whom was he collecting it for? A rival university? A black-market collector? Those religious loonies from last year's monkey trials? In any case, he surely wants money for it. Maybe he'll sell it to one of those entities, or maybe he'll hold it for ransom, expecting the University of Oregon to pay."

"No matter which of those might be true, we've got to get it back, and fast," Gunn said. She drained her coffee and stood up. With a finger in the air, she said, "To the sidecar!"

"It's far to Joseph, isn't it," Nell said to her half-eaten oatmeal.

"It is far," Gunn confirmed, "but we are fast!"

"And I'll have to ride the whole way in that sidecar."

Gunn nodded. "To assuage at least one worry, the Harley-Davidson and sidecar are quite safe. Read the *Oregonian* every morning and see how many car accidents happen. They report one every day on the front page. Never have I read an account of a Harley-Davidson with a sidecar being in an accident, especially not one driven by a flapper. Especially not a flapper with years of practice in the saddle." She waggled her eyebrows, and Nell rolled her eyes.

Gunn slid the front section of the paper next to Nell's oatmeal bowl. She tapped an oval fingernail on an item toward the bottom of page one in a box entitled "Day's Worst Accident in City Traffic." The eighteenth traffic fatality of the year, Nell read, occurred when twenty-seven-year-old Margaret Winesburg lost control of her car after a night of drinking and was thrown to her death. It ended with a stern lesson from Captain Frank Ervin of the police traffic division: "Whiskey and gasoline will not mix." Nell scoffed. They would mix, in fact. They were perfectly capable of forming a solution. People were so ignorant of basic scientific principles.

Nell was perking up, thanks to the strong, percolated coffee. Her mind's gears were engaging again on the main problem; the sidecar was a distraction. "The thing is, there's something unusual about the skull, and I—"

"How you do go on," Gunn drawled, finally looking up from the newspaper. "If you keep talking, we'll never get that skull back."

To the sidecar, Nell thought. "I'm still wearing yesterday's clothes, so I'll clean myself up, though I'm not sure why. That sidecar does not do wonders for skin, hair, or cleanliness."

While Nell washed up in the bathroom, Gunn washed up their breakfast dishes in the kitchen. When Nell emerged a few minutes later, Gunn was gone, but the back door was open. Nell stepped onto the back stoop and spied Gunn rooting around in the garden shed in the back yard. Before Nell could ask what she was after, Gunn turned around in triumph, a spouted metal can in her hand. "Gasoline!"

Gunn filled the tank and stashed the can on the front porch. Then with a twist of her wrist, they were off again. They wound back through Glenwood and the sunlit rather than lamp-lit streets of Springfield. Gunn stopped at a filling station to top off the tank with another half gallon of fuel.

As they drove out of town, Nell felt that this time, they were properly on their way. They tooled along through the damp morning in the long shadows of tall, dark-green pine trees. Depending on the curve of the road, the sun was either directly in their faces, warm and blinding, or just to their right, behind the trees. The dew hung heavy on the needles and ferns in the shadows, but the sun quickly lifted the drops as soon as it touched them. The air smelled fresher and cleaner as it rushed into Nell's nostrils than she remembered any air smelling. On her parents' farm in upstate New York, they had kept a few cows and chickens and pigs, and grew corn, soy, and hay in the fields out back. It wasn't a large farm—they sold the crops to farmers with whole herds of dairy cows for winter feedstock—but like all farms, it had an odor. It smelled of fresh mud and coming snow and burning brush and roses that her mother had planted under her bedroom window, but it also smelled of damp cows and chicken droppings and manure spread on the fields and the gasoline belches of the tractors. She'd spent the past few years in New York City, which smelled like people and everything they do. Garbage left out for pickup, automobile exhaust, Italian restaurants, Jewish delis, perfume wafting about the befurred ladies going to the opera. For Nell, New York City really smelled like ancient dirt and labs attempting sterility, students who didn't have time or money to wash themselves or their clothes properly, and the dryness of textbooks. This road, as it neared the small town of Thurston and led away again, smelled like the word "crisp" and the way it snapped at the beginning and came to a soft close at the end.

Walterville, Leaburg, Vida, the aptly named Blue River: Nell and Gunn rolled through each little town, where the pine trees parted for a mile or two to allow for a few houses and a general store, maybe a gas station with a mechanic, and ever more stunning views of the snowcapped mountains ahead. Rocky knolls covered in pines hid and revealed, depending on one's perspective from the road, the very white, very pointy tops of volcanic mountains. Thanks to her geology studies, Nell knew how the Cascades had formed, how the range was part of a line of volcanoes from Canada to California, each one ancient and yet poised to blow at any second and destroy towns up and down the Pacific coast. The danger made seeing their peaks more powerful, she thought.

By the time Gunn downshifted at the sign welcoming them to the town of McKenzie Bridge, they'd been on the road for a couple of hours. Nell's stomach was burbling as loudly as the Harley's engine. They were at a higher elevation now; Nell knew they'd been climbing since they'd left behind the Willamette River at Springfield's western boundary. The air was cooler here, but the sun was doing its level best to pour on the heat. By afternoon, no elevation would escape the sweltering wave.

Gunn pulled the motorcycle into a gas station and shut off the engine. The sudden silence disoriented Nell. She opened her jaw wide and popped her ears, which didn't help. Her cheeks felt as if a hundred spiders had been spinning webs across her face all morning. She brushed them away with cool hands, but that didn't help either.

The women took off their helmets and shook out their hair—Gunn's glossy bob falling neatly into place against her diamond-cut cheekbones, Nell's rough curls struggling to return themselves to the third dimension. Gunn swung her leg between Nell's head and the bike's rear tire to dismount, then she stretched from tiptoes to fingertips and let out an explosive breath. Nell opened the sidecar's little door and steadied herself against its sidewall before she attempted her exit. The sole of her right shoe scraped on the edge of the car, and the instep of her left shoe got caught as she dragged it out to join her right. Every muscle from her hips to her feet was buzzing, thanks to the vibration of the engine and the tires on the road. She mimicked Gunn's stretch and nearly got stuck in the full extension as her back spasmed. Nell quickly relaxed, knowing that next to Gunn the sleek setter, she looked like the last puppy in the pound.

"Hungry?" asked Gunn as she brushed a fine layer of dust from her smooth pink cheeks. "It's a gas station, general store, repair shop…I think they might even still shoe horses out back. If you need to see a man about a horse."

"I do not. But I am hungry, and a restroom would be nice." Nell's freckled cheeks were covered in a coarser layer of dirt, probably because she was closer to the road in the sidecar, or possibly because dirt didn't dare adhere to the porcelain skin of Miss Flagely.

A man in a grimy undershirt and ancient overalls came toward them from the general store. As he neared the motorcycle, Nell could see that the shirt was gleaming white between the black smudges. It was as clean as a gas station attendant—or his wife—could possibly get it.

"Howdy, Miss Flagely," he said with a nod. "You need a fill-up?"

"I do indeed, Fred. Ran out of gas last night, and I don't want to repeat that performance." Gunn removed her gloves. "We're going to pop into the store for luncheon provisions too."

"Ladies shouldn't even be driving infernal machines like this, let alone at night. And running out of fuel!" Fred shook his head at the horrors that could have happened, but Gunn let his admonition run off her tweed back. He twisted off the fuel cap with grease-blackened fingers, then turned to watch the gasoline fill the globe atop the pump. "I'll come in and tell Mabel the price when it's full."

"Thank you," Gunn said. She strode away, leaving Nell to trot after her as best as her cramped body was able. "Fred means well," she said to Nell when she caught up. "But Mabel…" She trailed off as they stepped on the plank porch and into the cool, dim interior of the general store.

The woman who must be Mabel stood behind the counter to the left of the door, throwing poisoned darts with her eyes. Nell waved the invisible darts away as if they were a swarm of gnats near her ear and smoothed her hair into a more acceptable shape while she was at it. She noted that the darts weren't meant for her, though. Mabel was aiming for Gunn, who sashayed down the narrow aisle, perusing the canned goods and bags of dried beans at her catlike leisure.

"I don't think Mabel likes you," Nell whispered.

"You don't say," Gunn said. She glanced up at Mabel, who looked out the open door at Fred pumping Gunn's fuel. When Gunn returned her gaze to the groceries, Mabel returned her gaze to Gunn. "When your husband is kind to the footloose anthropologist who writes about sex, you probably aren't going to accept that anthropologist into your sisterhood."

Gunn gave Nell and herself a good going over before proceeding past the sacks of flour and sugar. "We're also wearing trousers and men's footwear while riding a motorcycle unescorted across the high desert of Oregon."

"Let's not even tell them that it's a scientific mission," Nell said. "With our tiny female brains and all." She'd heard all about the difference in men's and women's brains over and over, and yet she'd managed to earn a professorship and devise a new method for dating human remains despite her brain size. Nell, as she had been told by suited men holding illicit whiskeys on ice in so many university drawing rooms, was the exception that proved the rule. Their incorrect use of the phrase set her teeth on edge.

"Run into a few Freds and Mabels yourself, eh?" Gunn said. The women examined the summer berries on ice in the back of the store. "People don't appreciate women on a caper. Or wearing men's footwear. Or the fact that we're women doing things in the world at all. In order to follow your passion—especially if your passion involves a dead person whose bony head was stolen by a man in a black hat—you've got to put up with some dirty looks and being thought unladylike. You've got to leave the lab and cross the desert." Gunn walked to a shelf stacked with loaves of crusty bread. She considered her few options and tucked one under her arm. "You're a bit of a trailblazer out here, Nell. This road we're on was just finished this summer, and it's the only road across the Cascades between Eugene and Joseph."

"We studied the Cascade Range in 'Geology of North American Mountain Ranges' my junior year," Nell said brightly, forgetting for the moment about Mabel's disapproving gaze. "They're actually a string of volcanoes from Canada to California, including Mount Hood, Mount Rainier, Mount Shasta, Mount Saint Helens—"

"If you like volcanoes, wait till you see what's coming up after lunch. You'll have a conniption."

Nell was caught halfway between intrigue and fear for her life. She figured these two states were unknown to Gunn. Nell picked up a little wedge of cheese with a waxy red rind, while Gunn grabbed a pint of small, bright-red strawberries.

They turned the corner at the end of the aisle and headed for the counter. Fred had come in, and he was leaning on an elbow propped near the cash register. "Twenty-five cents, Gunn," Fred called. "Mabel will ring it up for you." He jerked a thumb in his wife's direction, and she shied away as if he'd poked her with it.

"Good afternoon, Mabel," Gunn said pleasantly. She put the food on the counter.

Mabel looked at the women's smiling, dirty faces and dusty shoes. She did not return the smiles.

"Mabel's not much of a talker," Fred said by way of apology. "But she's great with a cash register. Good head for figures."

"That's quite enough, Fred," she said in a pinched voice.

"Aw, I bet you are great with a cash register," Gunn said. "Women are always selling themselves short, especially in business. Mabel is aces at running this store," she said to Nell.

"Don't you charm me, Gunn Flagely," Mabel said, though she couldn't stop herself from moving the pile of food nearer to the register. "I'm not one of your *subjects*."

"She knows your work," Nell said.

"Everyone reads Miss Flagely's work," Fred said with a wide grin. "She's famous."

"*Infamous,*" whispered Mabel as she rang up their lunch. "These strawberries are fifty cents a pint. You know that?"

"Yes ma'am. I read the sign," Gunn answered.

"Expensive," Mabel muttered.

"I can afford it," Gunn said. Nell could sense she was getting a bit testy. She wondered that it took this long to get under her smooth skin.

"I bet you can," Mabel said.

"Of course she can," Fred said too loudly. "She's a famous author. She probably sold a million of those books."

"Not quite a million," demurred Gunn. "You have them all?"

"Not all," Fred admitted. "Mabel won't let me have 'em in the house. My brother, he's got a ranch over outside Redmond, he's got 'em all. He lets me borrow 'em when a new one comes out, after he's finished it. Fascinating stuff, Miss Flagely, and from an Oregonian too. We're all proud."

"Not all of us," Mabel said. But her role as proprietor of a general store was too ingrained to keep her from her duties. She had rung up the items and put them in a sack with the top folded and sharply creased. She really was good at running the register. "That'll be one dollar and twenty-three cents, including twenty-five cents for the gasoline."

Gunn paid with exact change. "Thank you," she said with a nod to both Mabel and Fred.

Nell picked up the bag, but their egress was blocked by four broad-shouldered men in dirty plaid shirts and cork-soled boots. They were laughing and punching each other's arms as they moved toward the dim doorway of the store.

"Gunn!" the one with the longest, wildest beard exclaimed when he noticed the women in their way. "I haven't seen you in a coon's age."

"Robbie! So good to see you. How'd you escape from the forest?"

"Are these loggers? *Wobblies?* I've read about them in the papers back East," Nell said quietly over Gunn's shoulder. The engine being mounted so closely to her left ear had given Nell a false sense of what "quiet" might be, though. All four men looked at her.

"We're flunkies," said Robbie. "And Wobblies."

Nell frowned. "Flunkies?"

"Errand boys," Gunn explained. "They do all the work for the loggers in the camp while the loggers do the logging. Somebody has to get the groceries and cook the food and clean the place up. There aren't that many women in camp."

Two of the flunkies pushed past the crowd at the counter to do their grocery shopping while the first man asked Fred to fill up their truck's tank.

"This is Nell Kelly," Gunn said to Robbie. "She's an archaeologist visiting from New York. She's usually cooped up in a lab looking at old bones. I sprung her."

"Actually," Nell said, "I'm an archaeological scientist working on an experimental process of using dendrochronology in conjunction with geology and a bit of chemical analysis to better pinpoint—"

"You count the rings of the trees?" asked the smaller, thinner man.

"I do use the rings, yes," Nell said, pleased that he guessed correctly. "It's actually much more complicated, but yes. In this area Douglas fir provides an excellent historical record."

"Hey!" said a third man from the back of the store, near the cheese. "We're logging Doug fir! You could use our trees in the conjunction with the pinpoint."

"That's very nice of you to offer, but the trees need to be from the site where the bones were dug up."

"Those the old bones out in Joseph?"

"Yes!" Nell was again pleasantly surprised.

"We know a team out there. We can send one of the new flunkies out to get them word that you're coming and that you need a slice of a real old tree."

Fred came back inside, wiping his hands on a threadbare rag that he returned to his back pocket. "Did you say Professor Kelly as I was on my way out, miss?"

"Yes, I'm Professor Nell Kelly," she said.

"There was a guy looking for you this morning," Fred said. "He mentioned that he was looking for a Professor Kelly, from Back East. Needed to talk to him, he said, but this Kelly guy had left Eugene before he could find him. Had something of Kelly's. But he didn't look like no professor himself. Tall guy, scruffy, mean looking."

"It's him!" Gunn butted in. "The man in the black hat! I told you he was headed east, and as I said, there's only one road across the mountains. He hasn't figured out yet that you're Professor Kelly." She turned to Fred. "Did he say anything about me?"

"He did not," Fred said. "Just Professor Kelly."

Gunn looked perturbed.

"What was he driving?" Gunn asked. "I mean, surely you must know every make and model of every car on the road, Fred." This bit of flattery earned Gunn another volley of daggers from Mabel's eyes.

"A black Pierce-Arrow Model 48," Fred answered with confidence, "a few years old, but in good running condition. Maybe even some engine modifications. Sure was loud when he took off."

"Didn't need to be that loud at all," Mabel said.

"You're a doll," Gunn said to Fred.

Mabel snapped each of the flunkies' flaccid bills as they paid for their beer and groceries, then slammed the register drawer with a clang and a ding.

"We'll catch up with him after lunch," Gunn said to Nell.

"Anything we can do, Gunn?" asked one of the flunkies. "I don't like the idea of you two ladies riding around with a man in a souped-up Pierce-Arrow on the prowl. Sounds like this guy might be dangerous."

"He is dangerous!" Nell said. "He pointed a pistol at me." Everyone but Mabel seemed appalled at this outlaw's daring.

"There's nothing you can do right now," Gunn said to the flunkie. "You know I can take care of myself. And Nell here looks like a pale lab rat, but there's a strong and capable farm girl holding up that big brain. But if you see a Pierce-Arrow Model 48, run that sonofabitch off the road! He's got something that belongs to us, and we want it back."

"It doesn't belong to us so much as it belongs to science," Nell corrected. "You see, it's likely the oldest skull found in Oregon, even though it seems—"

"Though a little help in the anarchy department might be called for," Gunn interrupted, "if you're really sending a boy out to Joseph."

The bearded man hefted an imaginary baseball and tossed it to Nell, whose reflexes kicked in. She caught the empty ball of air.

The men laughed. Gunn said to Nell, "Might want to temper that reflex if a Wobbly throws something round your way, Babe Ruth. The International Workers of the World aren't known for tossing baseballs."

The flunkies headed to their truck, which was waiting in the dusty lot in front of the store. They put their groceries in the back and then sat with their butts crammed tightly together on the crummy seats in the four-man cab.

Gunn and Nell passed the truck on their way to a weather-beaten picnic table set in a patch of grass at the side of the store.

"You ever need anything, Gunn, you come back out to the show," said the driver with a wink. "We'll be movin' to the other side of the Cascades soon, most likely."

"Thank you so much," Gunn said. "It was most enlightening to spend time at your camp last summer. The book will be out this fall. I'll make sure to send a copy to the company."

"Better send it to the IWW bar in Portland. The company won't never get a book like that out to the men," the driver said.

"I'll deliver it myself," Gunn said with a wave as she and Nell headed for the picnic table.

"You girls take care of yourselves," cautioned the man squashed against the passenger side door. "Eastern Oregon ain't no place for ladies, even smart ones in trousers. Maybe specially smart ones in trousers." The men waved as they pulled back onto the paved road and headed east toward the fir-covered far slopes of the mountains.

Gunn gestured for Nell to take their lunch sack to the table while she retrieved the motorcycle from the pump and wheeled it in neutral to a shady spot near the table. Gunn popped open two bottles of Coca-Cola. Nell retrieved the food from its sack and used the paper bag as a placemat of sorts. They constructed simple cheese sandwiches for themselves and drank their soda pop in the sunshine, Gunn in long drafts, Nell in small sips. They ate the sweet berries in single bites and tossed the green tops into the grass.

"You wrote an ethnography about lumberjacks?" Nell asked.

"I did," Gunn answered, "but they prefer to be called loggers. Or flunkies, or donkey punchers. It depends on the job they do. Or Wobblies, if they're part of the International Workers of the World, and most of them are. The union bar is where they want me to send the book. I was part of a team of anthropologists studying the social structure of the camps a few years ago. One professor was creating a lexicon of logging-specific language, from tree terms to camp slang, like calling any logging operation 'the show.' One was studying social hierarchies. Whole families live at the show. They've got plumbing and everything out there. It's quite civilized. I, of course, was studying the sexual mores and taboos in the logging camp."

"But loggers aren't a people, like the Samoans; they're a job description. That's not anthropology."

"They're a culture of humans, and that's what anthropology studies, dead or alive, Persephone."

"I am not queen of the dead," Nell said around a mouthful of sandwich.

Gunn bit into her sandwich, swallowed, and continued. "Loggers have social structure and language and arts and rites and taboos, just like exotic natives in some South American jungle or on a remote Pacific island. And they are isolated from American culture at large for months at a time, working in camps in the deep Northwest forests."

"I saw the results of that isolation when I arrived in Portland," Nell said. "There were hordes of loggers and flukes and donkey divers or whatever you said stumbling around downtown. They didn't seem very family oriented or civilized."

"Says the unwed, childless archaeologist who doesn't leave her lab."

"Studying lumberjacks doesn't help our field become accepted as a hard science," Nell said. "Everyone thinks we're *sociologists*."

"Archaeology is 'harder' than cultural anthropology as far as science goes," Gunn conceded. "But if the science isn't hard, plenty of other things are."

Nell grimaced. "With lumberjacks? While you were studying them?"

"Loggers. And flunkies. And not all of them."

"You're not helping the field or the women in it one bit. How am I ever supposed to be taken seriously as a scientist when there are women like you and Margaret Mead mucking about in the name of cultural anthropology? Your lack of rigor—and let's face it, terrible reputation—could keep me from ever breaking the gender barrier at Columbia. How can I stand in front of the board across Broadway and convince them I'm not like you?" Nell brushed the crumbs from her hands and lap, crumpled the empty sacks, finished her soda pop, and stood.

Gunn drained her bottle and started walking toward the Harley. "I don't think they'll ever think you're like me," she tossed over her shoulder. "But how am I ever supposed to convince a closed culture to let me in if flat tires like you make all the women in anthropology out to be prudish bores? They can't tell the difference between anthropologists and missionaries, and most people do not like it when the missionaries come to town. A beer goes a long way in winning the trust of the natives. And given my area of expertise, a little something on the side is evidence-based science." She sat in the tan leather saddle and strapped on her helmet.

"It's unprofessional," Nell said as she climbed back into her sidecar and jammed her helmet over her curls—and her ears.

"It's unprofessorial, maybe, but writing about sex is my profession. I bought a house with it—Mohle House is mine. And those books keep my stately steed in feed." She patted the gas tank with her gloved hand. With a kick of her heel and a flick of her wrist, Gunn propelled the Harley eastward, up and over the pass.

9

In Which Nell Enjoys Geology and Artifacts

The Harley-Davidson's engine chugged and sputtered and made a big show of how very hard it was working to haul Gunn in the saddle and Nell in her sidecar up the western side of the Cascade Range. The evergreen trees thinned out along with the air, revealing a forest floor of brown needles between the junipers and the occasional patch of snow refusing to melt. The road wound up and up and up, switching back and forth in wide arcs that alternated with hair-raising hairpin turns. The sharper corners didn't have to be so harrowing, Nell thought as she swallowed her fear and a bit of her lunch. The motorcycle could surely go more slowly. Every left-hand curve gave Nell the sensation that she was hanging out in space over a precipitous drop, held aloft only by the bolt that stuck this bullet-shaped contraption to the bike's frame. It was more terrifying than any ride at Coney Island, not that she enjoyed those rides either.

She didn't need an excuse to clutch a man's arm, nor did she want to be soothed by said man. The little door of her sidecar flew open, and she snatched at it to shut it again, as if that flimsy piece of metal would hold her in place against the lateral g-forces created by Gunn's driving. A glance at Gunn's curled red lips told her she'd better hang on to her seat and keep breathing rather than make any attempt to get Gunn to back off the wide-open throttle.

A few dizzying minutes later, the spindly tree trunks were spaced wide apart, and the summit seemed to be a few feet away. Then a few more feet. Then it seemed to Nell they'd never reach the top; the road kept rising forever between the twisted juniper and scrawny pines, with the blue sky hung like a painted Hollywood backdrop between them. Nell glimpsed a sign reading "McKenzie Pass, Elev. 5325" as they whizzed past.

They rolled over a little hump and rode along a nearly flat patch of road for a minute or two before beginning the descent. Nell wondered if it would be better to close her eyes or keep them open. She decided to try sixty seconds of each and note the results on the clipboard in her mind. Hoping eyes closed was the correct answer, she tried that first.

She hadn't finished her first minute of the first phase of her experiment when the engine of the motorcycle slowed and the bike rolled to a stop. Nell looked sharply up at Gunn, who was unbuckling her helmet. Gunn gestured with her chin over Nell's head, and Nell followed her gaze.

Spending the past nearly forty-seven seconds with her eyes closed in scientific inquiry had been a mistake, she realized. Opening her eyes produced an unexpected nausea.

Also, they had apparently, in that short amount of time, been transported to the dark side of the moon. Rough waves of black rock surrounded them on every side, except for the road and its shoulder. A few brave trees and sturdy lichens clung to the stony sea at the top of the world. Nell hurried out of her sidecar and crouched to touch the rock without removing her goggles or helmet.

"It's lava," she said in amazement. "It's centuries-old lava flows. These mountains are extinct volcanoes, and this is from an eruption more than a thousand years ago."

"I thought you'd like it," Gunn said. "It's old and boring to most people." She still wore her helmet with the straps dangling by her ears, but she'd pushed the goggles up onto her forehead. "Can you believe this was a wagon trail? They had to cut through the lava. Once it was done, everybody used it, and now it's the John Day Highway, but for a long time, people tried every way possible to get over these mountains without having to deal with this abrasive black mess."

"It may be boring to you, but this is like looking at history. It's as if you went to Philadelphia and instead of looking at a bunch of old oil paintings, the Founding Fathers were forever signing the Declaration of Independence."

"Also boring," Gunn said with a flip of her hand. "Like bones."

"Then why did we stop?" Nell stood to face Gunn.

"I told you, I thought you'd like it. And unlike some people, I like living humans, even scientific ones who say mean things about my sidecar, despite the fact that its seat leather is starting to fit her lovely rump like a glove. Oh, don't get sore, Nell," Gunn said, flicking Nell's stiffened shoulder with the tips of her fingers. "I am glad for an adventure, whatever one I find. To the sidecar!" Gunn went back to the motorcycle and began reattaching her headgear.

"But we just got here." Nell looked around. She could see nearly 270 degrees from this spot, every direction but the one they'd come from, where the pass rose behind them a little and blocked the view of the valley on the other side. To the south were three broad, connected peaks with another smaller peak nearby. "Are those the Three Sisters?" she called to Gunn.

"Yes," Gunn called back from her saddle. "Creatively named North, Middle, and South."

"What's that other peak?" Nell asked, pointing.

"The Husband. Can we go now?"

Nell pursed her lips in proper schoolmarm fashion. "No, really. What's its name?"

"The Husband," Gunn said. "Really. Look it up, Professor."

Nell shrugged and looked north, where she could see two more peaks. She pointed and asked, "What are those?"

Gunn sighed and slumped over the handlebars. "The nearer one is Mount Washington, and the farther one is Three Fingered Jack, surely a friend of the sisters but not the husband."

"Don't be disgusting, Gunn." Nell turned away from the motorcycle. The sun warmed and softened the back of her brown leather jacket in the cool air of the summit.

"What's disgusting about Mount Washington? You brought up the Founding Fathers."

"You know what I mean." Nell walked back to the sidecar but didn't get in. Though she was genuinely interested in the volcanic peaks around her, she was also genuinely interested in putting off the inevitable race down the back side of the pass.

"It's really called Three Fingered Jack. There's a saloon at the bottom of the hill, and you can ask any cowboy in there what these mountains are called. They'll be happy to tell you."

"Because cowboys are such studious observers of geological phenomena and they live to share their knowledge."

"I can see why you pal around with dead people and rocks. Your social charms are quite affecting." Gunn fired up the engine, which was loud enough to drown out any further delaying questions and awkward conversation. "Now let's go get that skull!" she yelled.

Nell climbed in, pulling hard on the straps of her goggles and helmet to make sure they were tight. She made sure the leather loop of her stupid little door was secured by the toggle inside the sidecar. She gripped the sides of her seat, gritted her teeth, and wished she believed in God more than gravity.

Gunn leaned over the handlebars as she kicked the bike into gear, her elbows bent at crazy angles and leading with her crazy grin, though she kept her lips carefully closed against insect intruders. Nell felt as green as the fir trees as they careened around corners all the way down the mountain. Gunn only occasionally tapped the brake, offering one shouted explanation during a moment of relative quiet: "If I use the brakes, they'll burst into flames!" This seemed to be a feature in Gunn's mind, not a dangerous drawback. Nell could see the front brake glowing a faint red even with so little application. Every time a car came chugging up in the other lane, which luckily was a rare occurrence,

Gunn had to rein in her sweeping attacks on the corners
to allow the car room to pass the motorcycle in relative
safety. Nell could see through the windshields that the
drivers of the automobiles clutched their steering wheels
and grimaced in their attempts to avoid the drab green
contraption hurtling toward them.

Nell found that afternoon in a sidecar on the eastern face
of the Cascades among the needled trees, which were grow-
ing denser and taller the lower the elevation, was freezing
cold when careening down a mountain. The air had been
barely warmed by the morning sun before it went up and
over McKenzie Pass, and it couldn't penetrate the dense
green canopy over the tight twists that led them down the
mountainside. Nell wondered what frostbite on a person's
cheeks looked like. She wondered if the red of her certain-
to-be-bursting blood vessels, thanks to the elevation, speed,
cold, and sheer terror of this motorcycle ride, were coun-
teracting the green tinge of her motion-sick countenance.

It took too long and no time at all to reach the lower
elevations of the Cascades. Nell realized that the brown
splotch she'd been glimpsing between the trees was a little
town, and they were headed for it. There were a few roads
visible from the mountains that converged on the town, but
nowhere to go from here but down its main street. There
was a clear little lake near a butte to the north, but not much
else around for miles. The green trees of the Willamette
Valley had all but disappeared, leaving fields of grass and
grain to roll along the high desert, with an oasis of tall firs
among the buildings in town.

Gunn coasted down a street lined with a few wood-faced
buildings fronted by a covered boardwalk that seemed a

bit drunk and reeling, even at this hour of the afternoon. Gunn swerved into a filling station, cut the engine, and removed her helmet and goggles.

"I could have shut the engine off completely coming down that road!" Gunn said. "There was hardly a soul up there today to run into. We had the run of the width of the road, taking the turns at the apex. With you in the sidecar, those inside hairpins were like something outta Coney Island. The extra weight took down our top speed, but on a ride like that, you're not going to bury the needle anyway. It's all about finesse. Did you feel it? And did you see the looks on the other drivers' faces?"

"I felt sick."

"You look sick. Why are you slapping your face?"

"Frostbite. Spider webs. Hope that this is all a dream."

Gunn frowned with concern. "Did the altitude drive you insane?"

"You, Gunn, have literally driven me insane." Nell climbed from the sidecar.

"You've got a night to sleep it off. I did have to use the brakes a bit, so they're red hot and likely to warp. We'll give them an evening to cool down. You may have noticed the smoke coming from the wheels toward the bottom of the mountain."

"I assumed it was from the demonic hellfire that follows you around."

"If that were true, it wouldn't have been coming from the front of the bike." Gunn waved at the station attendant, who came out to service the bike, then took her lipstick from her pocket. She bent to the round mirror on the handlebar to reapply. "I'll take care of the motorcycle so it's ready in the morning; you head up the street to the Three Sisters Saloon and get us a room. It's on the right just up there. You can't miss it."

Nell took her satchel from the sidecar and walked in the direction Gunn's finger pointed. She could hear Gunn turning on the charm as the young man who worked at the station neared her. Nell imagined her shaking her shiny black bob in the sun and smacking her newly rouged lips to dazzle the poor man into doing repairs for free—or in exchange for a favor. *Wink.* Nell hustled away along the covered boardwalk before she could be thrown into the bargain.

From the shade, it was easier to see the brightly sunny street without squinting. Where the mountains had smelled of crisp needles and newly melted snow, this roadside stop smelled of dust and dryness so strongly that Nell felt the need to blow dirt from her nostrils. She couldn't, of course, not in public, and not without a handkerchief. The sun reached the street without seeming to pass through any filter; its light was likely as cold and unforgiving in winter as it was bland and hot in the summer. She imagined it bouncing off drifts of snow in the street the way it bounced around in the dust now. Either way, it was hard on the old optic nerve, Nell thought.

She refocused her gaze in the shade. It took a moment for the storefronts along her right to lose the blue tinge that things take on after looking too long at the sunshine. She passed a small, quiet general store, a saloon with several girls in slinky, dusty slips and tattered feathered headbands lounging on chairs and watching the open doorway like hawks, and a fabric store bustling with chattering women in plain house dresses and dusty shoes. She stepped off one walkway, crossed a side street, and hopped onto another boardwalk. Here was a large tack shop, complete with saddled horses tethered loosely out front. The smell of leather and wool wafted from the open doors. It was surprisingly pleasant, the smell of a barn without the stench of the animals. The tack shop took up this whole block; at the end of the walkway was another side street, a restaurant, and beyond that, not much else. A few houses, a few silos in the distance.

Nell stopped and frowned. How could she have missed the hotel? She turned on her heel and gazed across the bright street to the storefronts on the other side. There was a post office with a hitching post and a parking spot out front. Beside it she was surprised to see a theater with vaudeville shows and movies too. Tonight, it was playing Charlie Chaplin's *Gold Rush*. She had seen the movie in the city and thought it funny and clever. Here, it might almost be a documentary of the winter months, if cattle were gold. Next to the theater was a hotel, one that seemed rather nice for a town so small. She crossed the street, kicking up puffs of dust with her brown brogues, and pushed open the hotel's heavy wooden door.

The elaborately carved front desk was on the right, with a row of cubbyholes behind for keys and mail. Across from the desk was a large fireplace with a hearth made of local stone dotted here and there with pieces of sparkling lava rock. Large racks of elk antlers were mounted on either side of the gray stone chimney, with smaller sets of mule deer antlers hung beneath. Tufted leather chairs were set near the fireplace with small tables nearby for drinks and playing whist and books and other signs of civilization on the frontier. Two ladies in dresses barely above their ankles and long locks tied up in elaborate braided knots sipped from cups and eyed the unkempt blond in men's dungarees.

Nell smiled at the man behind the desk after she'd taken it all in. "What a lovely hotel," she said.

"Thank you," said the man, whose hair was parted on the side so precisely he might have done it with a ruler and slicked it down behind his ears. He wore a sharp, old-fashioned, narrow-cut black suit, not a garish, wide-shouldered thing like the city sheiks had taken to. His head moved up and down on his long neck as if it were hinged as he took in her mannish attire. His sniff told her she was not up to snuff, even in this one-horse town. Actually, she hadn't seen a single horse, only smelled their accoutrements at the tack shop. "Are you looking for a room tonight?"

"I am, for myself and Gunn Flagely." She walked to the desk and placed her elbows in the smooth, shallow grooves where countless elbows had leaned before hers.

"Mr. and Mrs. Flagely," he said as he lifted his pen and dipped it in the inkwell.

"No," Nell said. "Gunn Flagely. I'm Nell Kelly."

He shook his head a bit and shrugged his shoulders so slightly it seemed he had a tic. Recognition sparked in his dark eyes. "The anthropologist? Dr. Harold Flagely's daughter?" He repeated the shrug and added a sniff.

"You know her too? Even out here?" Nell couldn't hide her amazement. "Her reputation really does precede her. Anyway, I'm an archaeologist on the trail of the oldest skull in North America." She waited another spark of recognition at this revelation. She got only a downturn of his nearly nonexistent lips. "It's been stolen." Still nothing. "By a rangy man in a black hat with a pistol on his hip."

He recoiled in disgust. "I'm sure I don't know any such ruffian." He seemed to think everything she said, from archaeologist to pistol, was some kind of flapper euphemism.

"We'll be paying cash," Nell said, speaking the shared language of the New Woman and the old-fashioned man.

He looked at the ledger in front of him, which covered the width of the desk front to back with its leather-bound covers and creamy pages laced with neat, small handwriting. "We have two adjoining rooms with a street view. Will that be acceptable?" His tone indicated that nothing about Nell Kelly and this Gunn Flagely person could possibly be as acceptable as his rooms.

"That would be fine, thank you." Nell turned to look at the street while he made slow, careful notes in the ledger. He asked her to spell her name and then Gunn's name while she watched the slow parade of the occa-sional car and horse in the street pass by. None of them fit the description of the Pierce-Arrow they'd gotten in McKenzie Pass.

The concierge placed two keys with heavy, teardrop-shaped wooden fobs on the counter. At the end of each fob was an inlaid disk with the room number carved into it, 2 and 3 in this case. "Will you need assistance with your luggage, Miss Kelly?"

"Oh, no. This is all I have with me." She lifted the strap of the satchel.

"I see," he said with a sniff.

"We're anthropologists. Well, I'm an archaeologist. Miss Flagely is a cultural anthropologist. And the skull we're chasing down could change what we know about the history of mankind."

"Mmm-hmm." The man turned to his books and ran a finger along the ledger, as if he were looking for something—such as a way to seem busy and avoid Nell.

"I can't help but notice that you don't seem to approve of Ms. Flagely's and my scholastic and artifactual pursuits," Nell said. It had been a long, harrowing day, and she wanted to take it out on somebody. This sniffy guy would do.

"I have no opinion on what you and Ms. Flagely, or any women, do or do not do," he said.

"Oh, I think you do have an opinion. If Miss Flagely and I were here for an escape from our ignoramus husbands and snot-filled children, or to shop for provisions for the homestead, or to perform our societal duties with the ladies, that would meet with your expectations?" Nell turned to look pointedly at the ladies sipping tea. They were looking pointedly back.

"We often have wives of wealthy ranch owners stay in our hotel," he sniffed.

"But passing through on an adventure—on a motorcycle, no less! Did you know that? Did you hear us roar into town?—satchels in hand and wearing trousers, is not the business of a lady."

"You may conduct any business you like, as long as you do not conduct it in this hotel. There is a saloon across the street where women like yourself and your friend are welcome."

Nell read the meaningful gaze he leveled at her as if it were a picture book. "We do not do that kind of business. We are scientists."

"So you say," he sniffed. "I'm not sure that's a more appropriate occupation for ladies than what you'll find across the street," he said to the ledger.

Nell was about to set the record even straighter when Gunn burst in through the front door. Her hands were black with grease, and she'd smeared a bit on her cheeks. Her knees were dirty and her boots dusty, and she had the biggest bright-red grin Nell had seen on her face since they met.

"You got us a room here?" Gunn said, followed by an appreciative whistle as she took in the lobby.

"Two rooms," Nell said. She looked at the concierge, who was managing to give Gunn a once-over from top to toe all while looking down his long nose. A feat, really.

"Swanky. When I sent you to get a room, I meant the place across the street where I usually stay. The Three Sisters Saloon." Gunn said. The concierge harrumphed loudly. "I desperately need to wash up," Gunn went on. "The motorcycle needed a bit more than I'd anticipated, but Bucky at the station and I got her squared away. We had to take a few parts from his bin of spares, but we're set to ride in the morning when the brakes are cool as cukes." Gunn held up the knuckles of her right hand. The flesh nearly matched her lipstick. "Managed to burn myself."

The concierge's disdain at every word Gunn uttered posted her up on Nell's side of the argument, not that Gunn knew she had even taken a side in the fight. The two ladies sipping tea clearly had taken the opposing side, but silent partners were not very useful in a verbal argument. There was only so much sniffing the ladies and the concierge could do to make their point before they had nasal hemorrhages.

Nell picked up the room keys and dropped one in Gunn's filthy hand. "You're in three. I'll take two."

"Perfect. Let's get cleaned up and go across the street for dinner and drinks and drinks and drinks. This place is a bit stuffy and dry for my taste, though I'm sure the rooms are lovely. Don't worry," she said to the concierge as she strode loudly past the desk in her seven-league boots, leaving dusty prints behind her on the buffed wooden floor, "we'll be quiet as church mice—when church mice drink too much and bring other church mice back to their rooms to do terrible things."

Gunn waggled her eyebrows at Nell and made sure the concierge saw her do it. Nell would normally dismiss this bit of silent-screen theatricality, but if it flattened the concierge's tires, she was game.

The sound of Gunn's high-laced boots striding up the stairs shattered the quiet of the high-ceilinged foyer; Nell's brogues clattered up beside her. Their rooms were on the left, and the bathroom was at the end of the short hall. Only one door of the six they could see along the hallway was closed tightly, which meant they had the place almost to themselves. After a quick stop in the shared washroom, Nell ceded it to the filthy Gunn. It was obvious who had the direr need for a tub.

10

In Which Nell
Gets a Head

Nell woke an hour later to a loud rap on the door. She hadn't realized she was asleep, nor had she realized how tired she was when she lay down on the clean white coverlet. When the door swung open without her bidding the knocker to enter, Nell bolted upright, expecting to see the man in the black hat. Instead, Gunn with her slick of black hair strolled into her room on bare feet. Not even stockings under her silk slip.

"What's the story, Hunky Dory? Have you come up with a plan for nabbing the dastardly thief?" asked a sparkling-clean Gunn. Her lipstick was firmly in place, as always, but the smudged kohl that had surrounded her eyes all day behind the goggles had been scrubbed off and replaced by neat black lines that extended nearly to the outer points of her plucked eyebrows, vamp style.

Nell's hands flew to her pillow-mussed hair. "No, I didn't. I meant to, but…I fell asleep."

"Me too. The bath I took was so warm and lovely. I recommend it." Gunn sat on the edge of Nell's bed. "But not now, of course. I'm starving."

Nell noticed that the sunbeams streaming through the gauze curtains at the window, while still bright and strong, were nearly parallel to the floor. A bright rectangle of orange-ish light hung on the scroll print of the faded wallpaper on the opposite wall. "What time is it?"

"Just after seven. We slept long enough that we should be up for a hot time in the old town tonight, right?" Gunn slapped the top of Nell's bare, dirty foot and stood. "Get cleaned up. Put on your slip and tell yourself it's a silk gown. This hotel is about as fancy as we're going to get on this ride, and you must be tired to death of wearing denim and leather. Meet me in the lobby. I'll be making eyes at the prude working the front desk. I might roll my stockings on by the fireplace." She offered a sample of her leer for Nell as she sashayed out of the room and closed the door behind her.

Nell pulled the ivory slip out of the bottom of the satchel, where it had been stashed along with her wallet, her notebook, and a pencil. It was a wrinkled mess, but not as filthy as the knit shirt and dusty dungarees she was sporting now. Gunn had probably hung her slip in the bathroom while she drew the hot bath to steam out the wrinkles. Gunn did have some kind of magical ability to put herself together, even while wearing a slip in a Wild West hotel in a town surrounded by mountains and high desert after driving a motorcycle for two days. Nell removed her traveling clothes and crammed the whole mess in her satchel, stashing it in the armoire. She put on the slip, smoothing it as best she could with her palms. The only shoes she had were the brown leather brogues, which were just large enough to flop a bit on her feet. Gunn would likely wear her boots, and she'd probably look fantastic in lace-up riding boots and a delicate slip in a way not even a Hollywood starlet could manage. Or it was entirely possible the woman would forgo shoes altogether. The thought was equally appalling and likely. Nell's specialty, fashion-wise, seemed to be the ability to look worn out and strangely dressed at the same time. She stood in front of the gilt-framed mirror and ran her fingers through her curls in an attempt at insouciance that missed its mark, then twisted her favorite pink lipstick up from its tube and painted it on. It was literally the least she could do, and it did have an effect. *Thank you, Max Factor,* she thought.

She took a step back and examined herself from the waist up, which was as much as she could see in the mirror hung above the dresser. The tiny straps of the makeshift dress only made her farm-worked shoulders look wider, though she hadn't lifted a bale of hay in years. Her small breasts poked at the flimsy fabric of the slip. She might as well be naked. She hunched a bit and folded her arms across her chest, which made her look like a surly man dressed as a quiff for Halloween. She flung her arms out in exasperation and put her brown leather coat back on for a bit of modesty, even if it was still hot as blazes. The whole thing was ridiculous, from slip to saloon.

She closed her door and locked it behind her. At the bottom of the stairs, she found Gunn draped over the arm of a velvet settee with a cigarette held lightly between her slender fingers. She drew delicately on the cigarette, setting the tip to smolder, then exhaled while pinning the concierge to his perch behind the front desk with her Egyptian-influenced eyes. Nell hated to ruin Gunn's fun, but by now she was feeling seriously hungry. If they didn't find dinner soon, her stomach would start to grumble, which could only add to her attractiveness. Not even in a one-horse town could she be the ingénue.

"Gunn, are you ready for dinner?" she asked as she plopped the heavy key fob on the concierge's desk.

"I could eat...*anything*," Gunn purred as she drew herself up from the sofa and extinguished her cigarette in the ashtray, all without taking her eyes from the very red-faced concierge. She sashayed to the desk—in boots without stockings and looking quite fine for it, Nell noticed—and dropped the heavy wooden teardrop of a fob onto the ledger. "We'll be back before you know it," she whispered.

The concierge involuntarily leaned in to hear her, then jerked back to vertical when he realized his mistake. "Snake," he whispered. *"Vamp."*

Gunn smiled and slowly turned toward the door, where Nell was waiting and willing her to hurry up with quick flicks of her hand. They walked out of the lobby and into the bright sunset. The purple shadow of the mountains crept toward town behind them. As they crossed the street, Gunn exploded with laughter, her performance complete.

"He probably won't give us back the keys to our rooms tonight," Nell said.

"He deserved it. He's terrified of women no matter what they do—work, fuck, read, write." Though Nell drew her breath in sharply at the casual use of such a taboo word, Gunn barreled on. "We do all of those things—well, I do— and I won't let that frightened little rabbit tell me what I can and cannot do as a paying customer. I'm sure the rabbit's never told a man on business that he suspected him of prostitution. I'm sure you've noticed that 'working girl' and 'working man' do not have the same cultural connotations in America today. Ah!" They had reached the wood and glass doors of the saloon. Gunn clicked her heels together, held open a door like a Fifth Avenue doorman, and admitted Nell with a sharp bow.

The ceiling couldn't be seen through the haze of smoke from cigars and cigarettes, and the floor was covered in sawdust and shells that crunched under their heels. "Peanuts and pistachios," Gunn called over Nell's shoulder as they walked toward the bar. A piano player near the unlit fireplace thundered out raucous old-time rags, and everyone talked louder to be heard over the rattle of the keys. There were more men in the room than there had been in the afternoon, and the women draped over chairs and along stair railings had taken their eyes off the doors and planted them on the nearest interested men.

"No table service," Gunn added, pointing to a hand-painted "Order Here" sign hanging over the bar. It had apparently served some time as a target for sharp shooters in training, judging by the splatter of chipped holes in the wood.

Gunn leaned on the bar and waved wildly at a musta-chioed man near the cash register at the other end. He waved back and gestured with an upheld forefinger that he'd be with her in a second, as soon as he took care of the pile of coins and wad of crumpled bills in his hand. He straightened the paper, held each bill to the light, and placed them in the open till, then dropped the coins in their compartments. When all had found a home, he approached Gunn.

"Cowboys always pay, but their money is in the worst shape American tender could possibly be in," the man said. "At least it's legit. Usually." He wore bands on his sleeves, like they did in the wilder days of the Wild West, and had a thick white mustache. He could play a saloonkeeper in the movies without bothering the costume department. He straightened his shoulders and shook his head to clear it. "Where are my manners? Hello, Gunn. It's been weeks since I've seen you. On your way to join your father at the dig?"

"It's lovely to see you too, Albert. This lady to my left is Daddy's latest archaeological find, Nell. He dug her up in New York City."

Nell shook hands with Albert, who said, "You look good for being one of the professor's finds. Normally, they're missing important parts, like skin."

"I'm an archaeologist as well," Nell explained. "I'm here from Barnard College to date the skull Dr. Flagely found. Or, I was here for that, until it was stolen."

"That skull's been stolen?" Albert asked as he poured amber liquid into two chipped glasses full of ice. He added a bit of Coca-Cola and put the glasses with paper straws in front of the women. "That piece of bone was the talk of Oregon when Flagely found it. I'm surprised anyone could even get their hands on it. Who would let some two-bit thief waltz in and steal a precious artifact like that?"

"It's a bit of a sensitive subject," Gunn said as Nell downed half of the drink in front of her and blushed from her hair-line to her neckline.

"Oh! Well, I'm sure he was better than two bits," Albert offered by way of apology. "Two dinners, ladies?" He looked at Nell's half empty glass. "And maybe another round to the table?"

"Yes, please," Gunn said. She took her drink, Nell took hers, and Gunn located a table in the middle of the room for them. "There's only one dinner here, steak and potatoes with cherry pie for dessert in the summer and apple cobbler in the winter. It's delicious, if you like those four things."

Nell did, and she couldn't imagine anyone who didn't. They clinked their glasses together more gently than the glassware in this saloon had any right to expect and drank to the Three Sisters.

"It's busy for a Wednesday," Nell said, looking around as she sipped through her straw. She hoped it was still Wednesday; the part of her brain that kept track of the days was rattling away in that sidecar. At least two men sat at nearly every round wooden table in the saloon. A few were eating, some had girls perched on their knees, most were playing cards, and all were drinking. There were pistols on the table and shotguns leaning against the wood-paneled walls. It wasn't quite the violent Wild West; it seemed to Nell that the men happened to have guns on them for whatever reason, legitimate or no, and then put them out in plain sight in a gentlemanly way while they drank with friends or wooed wild women. Her father and brothers (and even, on the occasions when the flower beds were under threat of rabbits or whitetail deer, her mother) had used shotguns on the farm, and these men had the same casual respect for their weapons. Unfortunately, they didn't seem to have the same respect, casual or committed, for hygiene.

Clouds of dust swirled about their rolled-up shirt sleeves and dungarees tucked into boots. Most of the men had a ring around their heads, like a pale halo of cleanliness, where their hats had flattened their hair and kept the dirt out while they were riding. Below that, dirt and weather staked a serious claim on their faces.

Gunn planted her elbows on the worn-smooth wood of the table and leaned toward Nell. "Most of these guys are cowboys, but some are shopkeepers and cattle doctors and farmers who grow feed crops. You can tell which is which by whether their boots are fancy-stitched and clean or broken in like a friendly horse that's easy to ride. Those gentlemen over there," Gunn pointed to a table in the corner where nearly every man had floppy hat, a broken tooth, a week-old beard, and despite all that, a girl on his knee, "are gold miners. Not rich by most people's standards, but they like to spend all they get at the saloon. There's a bit of a boom between John Day and Baker City. Nothing like Alaska or California—Charlie Chaplin's not going to make a movie about Sumpter, Oregon—but they're dredging for it anyway."

Nell turned a bit in her seat to take in the variety of life in the saloon. As she turned back toward Gunn, she froze and slowly lowered her drink to the table.

"What is it?" Gunn asked, looking from the miners toward the direction of Nell's frozen gray gaze, which seemed to be behind Gunn. "Is it the man in the black hat?" Gunn whispered excitedly.

"No, it's nothing." Nell picked up her drink again and belted the rest of it, then closed her jacket tighter around her waist as if she'd caught a chill. "I think this is our dinner." She smiled as Albert closed in on their table, plates stacked on one arm and two glasses balanced in the opposite hand. He held the drinks out for the women to take then set the plates on the table and drew napkins and utensils from his apron pocket.

"Can I bring you ladies anything else?" he asked, clasping his hands in front of his chest.

"I'd love another drink," Nell said.

Gunn raised her eyebrows and agreed. "If she is, I am. Make it two, Albert."

"Will do, ladies. Seems like this one's in for a big night." He jerked a thumb at Nell and twitched his mustache then bustled off, his heavy black shoes kicking at his long, black apron. His black-and-white striped stovepipe pants were visible as he walked away.

Gunn cut into her steak. Red juice swirled out and pooled under her baked potato. "I'm not slinging you over my shoulder and carrying you across the street after dinner, young lady. You have to stumble to your room like every other drunken flapper." She took a bite and pointed her fork in Nell's direction.

"I'm not a flapper," Nell said as she cut into her own steak.

"You sure can drink like one," Gunn said with admiration.

"I have spent the past few years in the city, where liquor can be had almost any hour of the day, Prohibition be damned."

"This may not be any New York City, but we do all right for ourselves in the wet department. And I'm not counting the famous rain, which you haven't even seen." She chewed on a chunk of meat while she thought. "Why aren't you a flapper, Coed Kelly? You're smart, you've got ideas, and you certainly aren't going to let any stuffy old husband tie you down."

"That's just it—I'm smart, and I have ideas. Flappers have neither. They just drink all night and read Lipstick's column in the *New Yorker* and do everything that everyone else does to try to shock one another. It's a strange world when being shocking becomes boring. We can't all be Zelda Fitzgerald." She looked pointedly at Gunn while she chewed.

"Don't you confuse me with Zelda," Gunn said. "That bitch is off her nut." Nell nearly choked on her potato, necessitating another long draft of whiskey and Coca-Cola. "I met her and Scott in Alabama and ran into the both of them again in Paris. Those two are wild! I was at a party where Zelda just took off her underpants and stuffed them in Scott's pocket. Have you read any of his stories?"

Nell had to admit she had not.

"Well, don't. You'll hate them. You'll hate every character in them, except maybe Nick Carraway in that new one, *The Great Gatsby*. But Daisy? Gloria? Rosalind? They're all Zelda, and they're all crazy, but that girl takes the cake. She is beyond the outré jazz baby and should be driven straight to Dr. Freud's couch and strapped down. You think I'm out there? You think Lipstick is out there? Zelda is around the moon."

"It doesn't matter," Nell said. "No matter how around the moon they are, no matter where they stuff their underpants, no matter how liberated they think they are, they all get married in the end, even Zelda Fitzgerald."

"Even me."

"What?"

"Married and divorced." Gunn let Nell chew on that, and her steak, for a while.

"When?"

"I'm twenty-seven, Nell, an old lady. I put on a good show and I wear it well, but I've been a flapper since Zelda was dancing with cadets in Alabama. I married my own well-meaning Scott when I was nineteen. His name wasn't Scott; it was Paul. Came from a good family, went to a la-di-dah school Back East, and on and on and on. But I was a bit much for the poor boy. I let him go before I ruined his very lovely life."

"You let *him* go?"

"I did indeed. Marriage isn't bad for some people, and I'm sure Paul found a lovely ex-flapper who was ready to hang up her heels and lower her hemline and have a few kids, just as you say. But once I found out about drinking, sex, and cigarettes, it was all over for me. Having my own career and publishing books under my own name—I like that too. Paul did not. He wanted a proper wife to take care of him, not herself."

"That's what I mean!" Nell said, raising her half-drunk drink. "Men do a smart girl no favors."

"You just have to ask nicely," Gunn purred. "But you don't have to marry them before you ask."

Nell blushed with the heat of Gunn's insinuation and the flush of the whiskey rising to her cheeks.

"Miss Kelly!" called a voice behind Gunn. While Nell tried to hide her already burning face, Gunn turned full around in her chair.

"Who is that?" Gunn asked Nell with a sparkle in her eye. "You know a cowboy?"

"It's no one."

"Don't lie to me, Naughty Nell Kelly," Gunn said with

a wagging finger. "Not only do I study sexual habits as they pertain to the cultural fabric, but I am, as you say, a flapper. Boys and sex and lies about either of those things are my territory."

Just then Albert deposited two more drinks on the table. "Yours, Miss Kelly, is from that young gentleman over there." He pointed over Gunn's shoulder. The redheaded young man waved and smiled.

Nell would never, for the rest of her life, stop blushing. She stared at the crispy potato skin left on her plate and said to Albert, "Please tell Casey I said thank you."

"I will, Miss Kelly."

"Casey, eh?" Gunn said as Albert left the table with an armload of empties. "So it is indeed someone."

"I met Casey on the train," Nell murmured to her potato. She picked up a not-quite-finished whiskey and finished it.

"Did you two…ahem…move to the rhythm of the rails?" Gunn leered as she chomped her last bite of steak.

"No! We had dinner together the last night before we pulled into Portland. He's from Montana. He's here to work on his uncle's ranch for the summer." She pushed her fork around the nearly empty plate. She wasn't hungry anymore, and she didn't want this latest round of whiskey.

"You know quite a bit about him for one dinner," Gunn said. "Go say hi! Say thank you in person for the drink. He seems very sweet. And cute."

"Don't patronize me," Nell said.

"I'm not. Go. Shoo. Go say thank you like the rule-abiding, polite, non-flappery woman you are. If you don't, it makes you seem coy and flirtatious. You hate coy and flirtatious." She waved Nell out of her chair and away from the table with the backs of her hands, as if shooing flies from pies.

Nell pulled her jacket around her waist and aimed herself in the direction of Casey's table, where he sat with a handful of other cowboys. It was only a few yards from her table with Gunn. She set her trajectory and watched her giant shoes crush peanut shells as she crossed the floor. When she reached Casey, she drew her gaze up and straightened her spine. She clasped her hands in front of her and willed her thumbs not to fidget. She willed the blush in her cheeks to subside. She was glad to note that there were no ladies of any sort draped over the men at this table, especially Casey. Yet.

"Hello, Casey. So nice to see you here, and so unexpected. Thank you for the drink."

"You're welcome, Nell. If you're surprised to see me, I'm downright shocked to see you. I thought you were spending the summer in a cold university lab." He smiled up at her.

"I was to be in a lab, yes, but a situation has arisen that requires me to travel, possibly as far as the dig site itself in Joseph, Oregon. We're not sure yet."

"A situation, huh? I love situations." Casey leaned back in his chair and hooked his thumbs in his belt loops.

Even Nell knew that this was a male display for the benefit of fellow males, pure primate behavior. She had endured the required cultural anthropology undergraduate classes. His fellow primates responded with hungry grins. Nell suddenly felt very much like the woman alone in the West that everyone had been so worried about.

But there was no time to fall into in feminine vulnerability with Gunn Flagely around. In a flash, she was behind Nell with two drinks in her hands and her satchel slung over her shoulder. "Casey Cowboy! I've heard so little about you." She set the drinks down and, with help from another young cowboy who was powerless to resist Gunn's gestured directions, dragged two empty chairs to the table. The other men shifted their chairs in the sawdust, and Gunn pulled Nell into the chair in front of her drink. "I've not heard a thing, actually," Gunn clarified. "How long have you known our lady professor?" She sipped her drink, her wide dark eyes fixed on Casey like a silent movie ham.

"Well, I just met her on the train a few days ago. I got on in Montana, and she'd already come more than halfway across the country."

"Fascinating," said Gunn. She set her chin on her fist and her eyes on Casey's face.

"You may not know much about me, Miss Flagely, but I know quite a bit about you, thanks to Nell. She talked quite a bit about coming out to Oregon to work with Dr. Flagely in the lab."

"You don't say!" Gunn looked at Nell, who sat silent as a freckled stone next to her. "She said nice things about me?"

"Very nice, ma'am. She spoke very highly of you and Dr. Flagely."

Casey was covering for Nell, and Nell knew it. So did Gunn. She may be a flapper, Nell thought, but Gunn Flagely was no fool.

"I think she was mistaken," Gunn said with a sidelong glance at Nell. "I'm far more trouble than she bargained for."

"Is that the situation Nell spoke of?"

"Situation?"

"Yes, she said there was a situation that kept her from working in the lab this summer. Are you the situation?" Casey smiled knowingly, and the men at the table smiled too.

"Oh, that," Gunn said, waving off their leers. "No. It's a sensitive matter. And quite technical, really. Scientific. Nell, why don't you enlighten these gentlemen about the situation."

"Well," Nell began, her eyes firmly fixed on her cocktail, "it started when a man out hunting—" here she managed to glance up briefly at the pistols on the table—"found a bone on the ground near Wallowa Lake. He could tell it was some kind of leg bone, but he didn't think it could be a cattle bone or deer bone or any other bone he was familiar with, so he contacted the authorities. There hadn't been any unaccounted-for deaths in decades, so Dr. Flagely was called in to confirm. He used his knowledge of the *Homo sapiens sapiens* anatomy to ascertain that the femur found had likely been in situ longer than, say, ten years, a hundred years, or even a thousand years. That spurred Dr. Flagely to mount a full archaeological excavation of the site, where they found most of a human skeleton. Now, I've been working on a technique that blends the latest advances in chemistry, physics, dendrology, and archaeology to..." Nell went on, and on, and on, until each member of her audience was staring deeply into the bottom of his empty glass. Casey signaled silently for another round, and Nell recognized it as a signal for her to wrap it up. She wasn't completely insensitive to others' lack of education, and possibly interest, regarding old bones.

"So, in the end, there was cranium with the body that turned out to be the oldest skull—"

"Oh, that old skull!" cried one of the men at the table. "We know about that. Everyone knows about that." The other men nodded and grunted and accepted the next round of shots from Albert.

"Did you know it's been stolen?" Nell said, indignant at having been interrupted.

"No!" Casey said. "By who?"

"A tall, skinny man in a black hat with a pistol."

"There's a man like that on every ranch," laughed the man who recognized her tale of the skull. "There's a man like that at every table in this saloon. Good luck picking him out of a crowd." Nell surveyed the men in the room, and it was true. There were skinny cowboys with black hats all over the room, as well as short cowboys, old cowboys, and, she had to admit, cute cowboys named Casey.

"Next round is on me," Gunn said in the silence that had fallen on the table. "While Albert is mixing, we'll be dancing!" She grabbed the nearest cowboy, a slender, dark-haired, dark-eyed man who fit Gunn's frame perfectly as they came together to waltz to the jangly old tune being played by the even older man at the piano across the room. Gunn seemed to be leading, which suited the cowboy just fine.

Casey took Nell's hand and led her to a clear spot on the dance floor near Gunn and her new friend. It took a few bars of jangly piano, but Nell's spine gradually loosened at the spot where Casey had placed his hand on the small of her back. She knew how to dance, but she had only gone to a few of the fraternity dances at school. She'd never, even on the farm, danced with a redheaded cowboy on a floor covered in sawdust and peanut shells to an out-of-tune piano in a saloon while wearing perforated men's wing-tip shoes.

By the time Nell had finished her third dance and yet another glass of whiskey, she had flung her leather jacket onto a nearby chair, broad shoulders and pointy breasts be damned. Gunn had climbed onto one of the sturdy tables and started a high-kicking Charleston, to the delight of most of the men and a few of the women in the bar. She nearly knocked several guys on the chin with the toe of her boot as she flung her feet out, and when she waggled around the perimeter of the table, anyone on the opposite side had to hold down the furniture to keep it from flipping. Casey went to the bar for two more whiskey-and-Coca-Colas for himself and Nell to sip, but Gunn had given up on the mixers and was downing straight alcohol from shot glasses brought to her by her admirers, of which there were many. As the night wore on, it seemed everyone from here to Bend had heard about the ruckus on the party line, and they had all come out to see the show that was Gunn Flagely. A few upright citizens seemed to have come expressly to stand against the wall with their arms folded across their chests and cluck disapprovingly, not that anyone could hear them over the music, shouting, and dancing feet, especially not Gunn.

Nell had passed from tipsy to drunk and was leaning more heavily than she'd have liked on Casey as they danced. Their dancing slowed as Gunn picked up her pace. The piano player hadn't played anything so lively since before the Great War. Nell became heavier with drink, while Gunn used it as rocket fuel.

Casey bent his head to Nell's ear as they danced so close her mother would be scandalized and amazed if she knew what her daughter was doing. "Anybody else out here in Oregon that you know, besides me and Miss Flagely?"

"No," Nell answered with a slow shake of her head. "The man at the gas station asked me that too. And the answer is still no."

"I'm going to turn us around, and you look over my shoulder at the guy in the corner. He seems to know you." He worked the two of them around, none too fast, so Nell could peer through the smoky haze at two men sitting at a small table in the corner. Wait—no. She squinted and the two men became one man. A feeble candle lit the silver stubble along his jaw.

Her eyes popped open. "The man in the black hat," she said. "*The* man in the black hat. Not just any old black-hatted cowboy."

"He's been staring at you ever since he came in," Casey said, turning her back around to face away from the stranger.

"When did he come in?"

"I don't know. Just before Gunn bought the last round for the table, probably."

Nell peered over Casey's shoulder. "He's got the skull with him," she said. "It's in that black bag that he's got on the table."

"The *Homo sapiens sapiens* cranium you came out here to identify?" Casey said.

"That's the one. Hey, you used the Latin!" Nell smiled and nodded carefully, so as not to dislodge the thoughts that were forming. "We've got to get that bag. Let's dance a little closer to him. No! Let's have Gunn make a diversion first. No! Let's tell your cowboy friends the plan so they can help. I'll make him sorry he called me a little girl. He didn't know he was messing with Sidecar Kelly. Though to be honest, neither did I, at the time."

"You are one of the smartest, talkiest women I have ever met," Casey said.

"Is that a problem?" Nell bristled.

"I don't mind at all," Casey said.

But before they could put Nell's drunken plan in motion, Gunn's face appeared inches from Nell and Casey's, which were themselves quite close. "The man in the black hat is here," she said with a feline hiss, "and he's after you."

"I know," Nell said, still looking at Casey.

"We've got to create a diversion," Gunn said, tapping a red nail on her red lip.

"I was just saying much the same to my friend Casey here," Nell said, still not looking at Gunn.

"Lookie here," Gunn said as she turned toward the front doors with a slow smile. "We might not have to do a thing. But keep an eye on the thief."

"I am," Nell said, still gazing at Casey.

A large woman in a long, gray dress and brandishing a heavy metal cattle prod threw open the front doors. A small army of angry-faced ladies stood behind her with sledge-hammers, hatchets, pitchforks, and any other handheld farm implement they could carry comfortably into the saloon. They all wore matching old-fashioned lace-edged white cotton caps tied atop their heads. Everyone in the bar fell silent. Nell finally tore her eyes from Casey's.

"It is nearly midnight, the witching hour, and you—!" The leader with the prod turned a gnarled finger and a squinting eye on the customers and bartender alike. "You are all doing the devil's work! Fueled by the devil's water!"

She lifted her prod over her head, and her friends hoisted their weapons with a "hear hear!"

"We are the Avengers of Satan's Saloons, and we are here to do the work of the Lord and the law. We aim to smash that bar and everything behind it." She walked across the floor until she was toe to toe with Gunn, then leaned forward until her pug nose nearly met Gunn's button nose. "You have not been observing a pious evening, Ms. Flagely. Oh yes, I know who you are. Everyone knows who you are. I don't know if you have ever had a pious evening in your heretical life."

"I have not!" Gunn said with affront. "And how dare you suggest I may have had even one pious evening."

"I won't make that mistake again," sneered the woman. "Ladies! Do your holy worst!"

The dozen angry ladies in long woolen skirts on a hot summer midnight roared and set to smashing. They whacked glasses with shovels and took hatchets to the bar. They tipped tables and hacked at the wood with hoes. The men were powerless to stop them, and the ladies of the saloon gathered on the stairs to watch and laugh at the evening's entertainment, the feathers in their headbands quivering. Albert stood behind the bar to protect the bottles, which were costly to replace, but let them have at the furniture. The resignation in his face told Nell that he'd repaired and rebuilt the tables and chairs often enough in recent years.

Nell caught a skulking movement to her right and remembered that she was supposed to keep an eye on the man in the black hat. She slowly pivoted her head and refocused her blurry vision in that direction. The man in the black hat, sometimes two of him, was indeed creeping along the edges of the room and making for the back exit under the stairs.

The leader of the Avengers of Satan's Saloons followed Nell's gaze. She took one look at his hat pulled low, his slinking walk, and the bag of something evil under his arm and pointed in his direction. "Ladies! We have the devil amongst us, and he is trying to escape!" Her minions roared again and a breakaway group of three Avengers set on the man, who went from slinking to scurrying along the wall as they gave chase.

The three angry ladies cornered him and seized the bag, but all he let go was a string of vile words, which only made them angrier. The ladies dug their heels into the wooden floor and leaned back, and the man gave the bag a quick jerk in an attempt to knock them off balance. It worked too well—all four fell to the shell-strewn floor with a thump, and the bag flew into the air.

"Nell!" cried Gunn.

Nell watched the bag arc in slow motion, then come down, down, down, and land gently in her outstretched forearms. She had not put her arms out to her knowledge, but there they were. Acting on the instinct of a girl with brothers, she tucked the skull under her left arm, stretched out her right, and made an end run for the swinging front doors.

A pistol shot rang out across the room, and everyone in the room hit the floor. Nell gathered the skull under her shoulders and looked toward the man in the black hat, but he had flattened against the floorboards just as everyone else had.

The gun belonged to a man at the top of the stairs with a thick black mustache and a wide-brimmed hat pulled low over his eyes. He was hiking up beltless pants that he may have just finished buttoning moments before. A woman with a sheet wrapped around her like a Grecian goddess stood next to him.

"What," he asked, "in *the* hell is going on down there?"

"The Avengers of Satan's Saloons are here to do the work of the Lord and the law, Sheriff!" called the woman who led the band. She pulled herself off the floor, which signaled to the rest of the bar that it was probably safe to stand.

"Aw, Retha, I have told you a million times not to pull that nonsense here. Look at this place." Everyone did. "We have little enough going for us out here, why ruin the one place we have to blow off steam." He stroked his mustache and continued thoughtfully, "Though I guess you are blowing off steam in your own weird way. In any case, you've got to repay Albert for smashing his things."

"But he's flouting Prohibition, Sheriff!" Retha's minions roared in angry agreement.

"No one cares but you, Retha. Probably some of your ladies are secret tipplers." There was no roar from the ladies, but there was a lot of shoe examining among the Avengers. "Ah, Gunn Flagely. Good to see you." He tipped his hat, and Gunn curtseyed as he continued his survey of the room. He picked out Nell next. "You, miss. What is in that bag you're holding?"

"My knitting?" Nell said.

"Good answer," said the sheriff. "And you," he said when his eyes hit the man in the black hat, who was sneaking out a side door. "You are not conducting yourself in a manner to be above the suspicions of the law."

The man in the black hat froze, then straightened and placed his fingers on his chest as if to ask, "Who, me?"

"Don't give me that," said the sheriff. "What are you up to?"

The man in the black hat bared his pointy teeth like a cornered animal. All eyes were on him, and his eyes were on the side door a few feet away. Without a word, he pulled his pistol from his holster, winged the sheriff in the shoulder with one well-placed bullet, and sprinted out the door into the black night.

The befeathered women in the bar ran toward the sheriff, the men ran out the door after the man in the black hat, and Gunn, Nell, and Casey ran out the front door with a shrug and a skull. "You wanted a diversion," Casey said to Nell as they crossed the street to the hotel. "Doesn't get more diverting than that."

11

In Which Nell Encounters Skin and Bones

Again Nell found herself waking from a sound sleep in her hotel room bed, but things were very different this morning than they had been after yesterday afternoon's nap. For one thing, there was a tiny man with a gargantuan hammer pounding on the inside of her skull. He seemed to be forging horseshoes for a cavalry regiment, given the nonstop noise and effort that he was putting into the process. For another, there was a full-sized, real-life man next to her in bed.

Nell gasped and jerked away from him, clutching the sheet to her breasts. Which, she now realized, were naked. Her whole body was naked. And judging from the bare back and the way the bright white sheet draped over the bottom half of the man's slender, muscular body, he was naked too.

"Oh, hell," Nell whispered. She arched herself carefully over the sleeping man so she could see his face, which was turned toward the wall. She sighed with a measure of relief—it was indeed Casey. At least it wasn't some strange, dirty cowboy; it was a cowboy she knew, and the skin she could see on his back, face, and arms was clean and creamy, though there was a faint ring of color around his biceps and at his C7 vertebra that would deepen over the summer as he rode the fences.

She turned to her right to check the clock that sat on the nightstand and gasped again when confronted by another pair of eyes. It took her a second to register that these were the empty sockets of the skull she'd recovered, and she chuckled quietly at her shock. Waking up next to bare bones was far less unusual for Nell than waking up next to a naked cowboy.

She arched her body forward now, to see over the edge of the bed. Shoes, boots, a hat, a pair of jeans, a literal slip of a dress, and everything else either of them had been wearing the night before were scattered from door to bed. Nell felt horror and happiness slugging it out in the pit of her stomach like a Jack Dempsey fight. She closed her eyes and searched her memory. He'd used a sheath. Not ideal, but probably all right. The rest of what she remembered was more than all right.

She scooched herself forward a bit, careful not to disturb the deeply sleeping Casey, and leaned forward even more to see herself in the mirror mounted on the armoire. Holy horrors, it was awful. Her rough curls were lumped up on one side and flattened on the other, like a well-loved corn husk doll. Red wrinkles spidered across her cheek where she had fallen asleep on the crisp cotton pillowcase and stayed there without moving all night. Her lipstick was long gone from her lips, though a smear of it seemed to be clinging to her right cheek. Mascara pooled under her eyes, making the purple bags she was carrying even darker and heavier. A piquant aroma arose from her swaddled body. *Lon Chaney ain't got nothin' on me,* she thought.

How she would get out of bed to put on clothes without removing the sheet from either her own bare body or Casey's perplexed her. No articles of clothing were within arm's reach. She wondered if it even mattered at this point if he saw her in this state, given what they'd done together the night before. She decided it definitely mattered. One's uninhibited actions at night cannot have bearing on one's dignity the next morning. She slowly lowered herself into a crouch next to the bed and crawled quietly to the slip that had served as her dress, which she popped over her head as quickly as possible. It reeked of smoke and whiskey and sex. She had never wanted to wear dusty men's dungarees and a jersey shirt so badly in her life, but the slip would do for now. She rolled her puffy, smeary eyes at herself in the mirror and hustled to the bathroom to wash up—"top and tails," as the saloon ladies of last night might say.

Of course the bathroom was already occupied; it had to be pretty late in the morning, and she had no idea if any of the rooms besides her own and Gunn's held lodgers. *Gunn.* If Nell had a boy in her bed, how many men were in Gunn's? She was grateful when the man running the forge in her forehead pounded the image that had started to form out of her mind. She leaned against the wall in her smelly slip dress and waited for whoever was in the bathroom to come out.

Minutes passed, and Nell was still waiting. Her heavy head had tipped against the scrolled wallpaper, and she may have fallen asleep while standing, as horses do. She snapped to, pulled herself upright, nearly fell over in the opposite direction, and steadied herself. She planted her feet wide and held her hands away from her sides until she was sure of her balance, then she rapped gently—for her own sake as much as to be polite to the bath's occupant—and called softly, "Excuse me, but do you know how much longer you'll be in there?"

The door swung open and one of the women from the hotel lobby the day before emerged. She was shorter than Nell, yet managed to look down her nose at Nell's filthy silk slip. She sniffed at the mélange of odors wafting from Nell and curled her lip.

"Archaeology, by its very nature, is a dirty business," Nell explained as she slid past the woman and into the bathroom.

"Is that what you call it," said the woman under her breath.

"From the Greek *archaiologia*, the study of ancient remains; also the Latin *archaeologia*, meaning antiquarian lore. Yes, that is what we call it." She shut the door more loudly than she intended and sat down hard on the edge of the tub. She reached for the faucet and turned it on. The warm water flowing into the tub pounded her eardrums like Niagara Falls. She held her head in her hands while she waited for the tub to fill.

The door opened, and Nell looked up so quickly she almost fell into the tub while still in her slip. She'd forgotten to set the latch. She righted herself and focused her eyes on the intruder. She was relieved—and then annoyed—to see that it was Gunn.

"Please go away," Nell said.

Gunn was dressed in her tweeds and laced into her boots. Her lipstick was in place and her hair was its usual glossy black curtain. "No time for that, Late-Night Nell Kelly. The man in the black hat knows we've got the skull. We've got two scenarios: he either hightailed it out of town last night to escape the Christian mob, or he was hauled into the hoosegow for an overnight stay. In either case, there's only one road through this part of Oregon, and we're on it. As long as we're sitting still, we're sitting ducks."

Nell shut off the faucet and looked at the clean water with longing. "We're heading back to Eugene?"

"That's what he thinks we'll do," Gunn said with an emphatic twist of her index finger. "So we'll go the other way. We'll stick with your plan, Professor Kelly. We'll go see Daddy."

"Does heading further away from what little civilization there is in this state really seem like the smart thing to do?" Nell asked. She trailed her fingers in the warm water. She wasn't one to second-guess herself, but she had the skull now. And a banging headache.

"Don't be a snob; it doesn't suit you. Besides," Gunn tossed her words over her shoulder as she exited the bathroom, "Daddy's got lots more bones at the dig site in Joseph. But we've got to get a move on if we're going to fool the thief."

Nell splashed her face with the water in the tub and rubbed her arms and feet before releasing all that lovely warm water down the drain. She dried off with a little white hand towel, which was streaked with brown dirt when she dropped it into the laundry basket in the corner.

The door to Gunn's room was open as Nell left the bathroom. With a whistle that pierced Nell's skull and a jerk of her thumb, Gunn gave her beau of the moment the old heave-ho from her bed and her room. He got up to dress nonchalantly, giving Nell her second glimpse of a naked man that morning.

That reminded Nell of the naked man in her room, and she hustled to see if he was still there. She never thought she'd want to burn an article of clothing as badly as she wanted to burn this slip. It smelled like it was halfway to spontaneous combustion already.

Casey was awake in her bed and squinting in the bright sunlight. He was shaking out a match with one hand and holding a hand-rolled cigarette between his lips with the other. He inhaled, exhaled, and said softly, "Good morning."

"Good morning." Nell hovered just inside the doorway, unsure where to let her eyes rest. She settled on the floor and crossed her arms across her brassiere-less chest.

"Do you feel like hell too?" Casey asked, one eye crimped shut against smoke and sunlight.

"Yeah."

"Come sit down. I can't imagine trying to stand right now. You should get a trophy for being able to move." He leaned forward to pat the foot of the bed. She crossed the room, but he stopped her before she sat down. "Wait—could you, um, hand me my pants?"

Nell grabbed them from the floor, belt still strung through the loops, and handed them to him as if they were the fragile wrappings of a ceremonial burial. She could hardly bring herself to look at him or his pants as he took them.

"Thanks," he said. "I don't think I've ever asked someone to hand me my pants before." He turned in the bed and discreetly slipped them on under the sheet. He stood and faced away to button and buckle, cigarette dangling from a corner of his mouth. Nell stole glimpses of his wiry, muscled torso while his eyes were shut to keep the smoke out of them. When he opened his eyes, took the cigarette from his mouth, and turned to her, she quickly looked at the skull as if deep in scientific thought.

"I'll head down the hall to the washroom," he said as he squashed out the half-smoked cigarette, "to clean up a bit. You can get dressed yourself while I'm gone. Then we'll see if Alfred across the street has any breakfast for a couple of hungover beasts. Not that you're a beast, Professor Kelly, but you must be feeling it this morning." He kissed the part in her mussed blond hair and left the room with his remaining clothing and boots in his hands.

A very pleased Nell took off her slip and put on the dungarees, knit shirt, and jacket. She was tying her brogues when Gunn skidded to a halt in the doorway. "We've got to get out of here, now!"

"I know," Nell said. She stretched and threw her satchel over her shoulder. She patted the skull on its bony head and placed it carefully in the black flannel bag, then drew the cord at the top closed.

"No, now! Right now! There was a third scenario, but I was too feather-headed to consider it. That old wolf is craftier than I suspected. He's across the street, in the shadow of the covered sidewalk, watching the hotel. I saw the glint of his pistol in its holster. We've got to take the back way and get the Harley from the service station."

"But Casey will be waiting in the lobby," Nell said.

"It's the moment of truth, Nell Kelly." Gunn leveled her smoky eyes at Nell's bloodshot ones. "Who do you love—the admittedly delicious man you had sex with, or the dead man you traveled three thousand miles to meet?"

Nell clutched the black sack. "To the sidecar!"

12

In Which Nell Finds a New Hangover Cure: Hot Lead

The Harley-Davidson sputtered and lurched as Gunn wrestled it as close to the gas pumps as she could before it died completely. "Out," she commanded Nell, whose foggy brain obeyed without question. "I'll have to push it close enough for the hose to reach the tank."

Nell stood dumbly where she had removed herself from the sidecar. She had no idea where they were, other than the fact that they were a couple hours' horrid motorcycle ride from the Three Sisters Saloon. Two hours of motorcycle engine in her ear. Two hours of rolling fields and not a scrap of shade. Two hours to think. Two hours to stew. Two hours to picture that faint line of tan at the base of Casey's neck as he slept next to her in the morning sunlight. She had gotten drunk and danced the night away and fallen exhausted into bed with him. But not too exhausted, apparently, judging by their state of undress this morning.

Her face reddened with embarrassment and anger and too much sun and capillaries wanting to burst from the whiskey they'd had to carry through her bloodstream all night. It was hard enough for a woman to get ahead in this world without having drunken sex with men they hardly knew. Men were useless. Love was useless. Sex was useless, no matter what Gunn Flagely might say. She had to clear her head and focus on the man who mattered: Skully.

A grunt followed by a roar startled Nell, and all the blood that had rushed to her face drained instantly. She turned to find a black bear stood behind her, snarling and swaying its giant head back and forth, back and forth, mere feet from Nell's frozen body.

"Aw, he wants you to say hi," Gunn said, joining Nell near the bear while an attendant in matching blue cotton cap and coveralls pumped gas into the motorcycle.

"Hi," whispered Nell to the bear.

"Oh, come on, say a proper hello." Gunn nudged Nell nearer to the bear. "If you make friends, he'll eat the man in the black hat whole, won't you, George?" Gunn stepped in front of Nell and patted the bear on the snout. "Now, you stop making a fuss, Mr. George. Nell's a fine young woman. She's a scientist from Barnard College in New York City, which is pretty impressive, right? And she knows Franz Boas. And she slept with a cowboy last night. She would never admit it, but she's quite the flapper." Gunn gave George a conspiratorial bump with her elbow. "The owners of the café next door took this little guy in when he was a cub, his mother nowhere to be seen, his ribs sticking out like a fur-covered picket fence. They've kept him here ever since. He's chained up so tourists won't get too scared, but at night, he sleeps in their living room on a braided rug the missus made special for him."

Nell was not sure the keeping of bears as pets was a good – or even ethical – idea. She huffed and opened the satchel slung over her shoulder. She took the skull from its bag and held it level with her unsteady gaze.

"Gunn," she finally said, "have you ever done something you wish you hadn't done?"

"Well," Gunn left off scratching the happy bear's huge head. "I've done things that, when examined in the light of the next morning, weren't my cleverest ideas, but I don't know that I've ever regretted them. What are you regretting, Professor Kelly?"

"This is the man who's going to take me places. No other. And definitely not a cowboy." She looked deeply into Skully's dark sockets. "I shouldn't have slept with Casey last night. I'm smarter than that."

"Sleeping with Casey Cowboy does not make you dumb," Gunn said. "It makes you human. A *living* human. A human who needs a night of sex and whiskey every once in a while."

"But I'm a scientist."

Gunn scoffed and spit in the dust. George wrinkled his nose at her manners. "You are indeed a scientist, Dr. Kelly, even if you don't have tenure. You couldn't be anything else if you tried. Even scientists have to break out of the lab and do the Charleston sometimes."

"We go to dances and parties with the men from Columbia all the time," Nell admitted to the skull. "But it's not the same for women. We have to work twice as hard and be impeccable if we want to get be regarded as half as good and tolerable."

"Do you think Margaret Mead is impeccable?"

"No!" Nell turned to Gunn as if she were insane.

"And yet she's doing some of the most daring, inventive cultural anthropology to date at the Museum of Natural History in New York. When the work she's doing right now with the Samoans is published, it will change everything."

Nell said nothing rather than admit Gunn might be right.

"And do you think I'm impeccable?"

"No," Nell scoffed.

"And yet my work outside the very conventional and fuddy-duddy university system has bought me a house and the freedom to live as I choose. But you're right about one thing."

"I am?"

"I do work hard. And I work just as hard to make it seem as if I don't." She winked at Nell, who screwed up her face in perplexity. "I keep all the effort under wraps at Mohle House, in that train wreck of a downstairs study that I'm sure gave you the fits. The one with the fireplace and the papers tossed about as if a tornado was the interior decorator?" Nell nodded. "But when I'm out and about, I am the height of fashion and fun, Goodtime Gunn Flagely the flapper through and through, boy." She leaned in closer to Nell and whispered, "Do you know, when I'm working, not only do I not wear lipstick but...*I wear glasses.*"

Nell took a minute picture a plain-faced Gunn in glasses. It was surprisingly heartening. "There are no consequences for you," Nell said at last. "Your father is nothing but encouraging. My parents think this university thing is a fling, despite the time and money and dedication I've given to my studies. Every letter from my parents, every telephone conversation we can manage, opens a chasm that leads straight to hell."

"What, pray tell, is hell to a scientific-minded girl like you?" Gunn asked.

"The farm," Nell said in a voice as dull as dirt. "My parents have a boy and a barn all set up and waiting for me as soon as I get tired of the life of the mind."

"I take it you don't see the same pot of cow dung at the end of that intellectual rainbow?"

Nell snickered just a tiny bit. "I do not."

"If it makes any difference to you at all, I'm on your side," Gunn said, giving Nell a little chuck on her shoulder. George grunted in agreement. Or argument. Or hunger. Nell found George hard to read.

Nell rocked her head back and forth as she dithered and allowed herself at last to smile a little, despite the sensation that her still-drunk brain was floating about untethered inside her cranium. "It does make a difference to me," she admitted. "But why do you work so hard only to wreck your reputation the second you step outside the writing room?"

"I'm not wrecking my reputation. I'm making it. How could I possibly write about sex if I didn't seem to have any?"

"By that logic, I'd have to be dead." Nell looked at the skull in her hand.

"You've got a long way to go before that's the case, Ace, given what I heard last night."

"You heard us?" Nell's eyes opened wide. She turned her head too quickly, setting the little man with the hammer and anvil off on a new clanging frenzy in her temples.

"Oh, everyone heard, doll," Gunn said. "The hotel, the saloon, any stragglers in the street after we retired to our rooms. Oh, now, it's hardly worth making that face," Gunn said as Nell became pale with horror. "And it's hardly worth regretting having fun in a cowboy town with a cowboy like Casey. You've got your first love, Skully there, in the palm of your hand, so you chose according to your true scientific heart. No ranch-hand woman or farm-wife life for you. Now don't add to your list of regrets by passing up the opportunity to pet a tame black bear before we have to hop right back on that horse named Harley and hightail it for Joseph. We have to get going before the man in the black hat figures out we've gone the wrong way."

Nell stepped her right foot forward gingerly and leaned in to pat the bear on its soft little ear. George tipped his head into her hand, and Nell scratched a bit more bravely. His fur was dense and, near his skin, very soft. Gunn smiled and nodded at George.

"For a far-flung Oregon fling, you chose well, Nell Kelly," Gunn said as she petted the bear's head herself. "That freckle-faced boy is cray-zay about you, and not just because you got drunk and gave it up faster than a Duesie on a racetrack. He likes you for your mind, Professor. While you were delivering your little impromptu lecture at the start of the evening, he was lapping it up like a golden retriever."

The two women walked back to the motorcycle, where the attendant was waiting for payment and to give them a lecture on the dangers of two women traveling alone. Gunn pressed a few coins into his palm then saddled up. She kicked the motor to clattering life before the attendant could finish his admonitions, and they sped away, leaving him in a cloud of Harley-Davidson dust.

The Cascades faded into the background, leaving a surprisingly featureless stretch of road in front of them. It was
more like the tumbleweed-strewn Wild West of a Tom
Mix movie than the green piney jungle of the valley on
the other side of the mountains. The air was warming as
the sun climbed, promising that it would be very hot by
afternoon, with little shade to shelter them.

Nell turned her head to watch the wildflowers wave in
the breeze as they passed and to give her face a break from
the constant pummeling of air at forty miles an hour. She
swatted at a gnat that seemed to be hovering in her slipstream, near the corner of her right eye. It wouldn't go away.
She lifted the corner of her goggles to free it, in case it had
gotten trapped behind the lenses or under the strap, but
that didn't clear the little black speck from her peripheral
vision either. She finally twisted all the way in her seat to
see what could be behind her. It wasn't close, and it wasn't
a bug. It was a car. She peered at its windshield. The sun
was glaring off the glass, but she was sure there was a man
in a black hat driving the car.

Nell pulled on Gunn's tweed trousers and got an irritated
momentary glance for her troubles. She tugged again and
quickly jerked a thumb behind her before Gunn could return
her attention to the road ahead. Gunn frowned behind her
goggles and peered into her dusty rearview mirror. She saw
the car, and apparently she recognized the man driving it
too. Nell saw Gunn's red lips say "Shit" and her wrist twist
harder on the throttle. Gunn was already pushing the Harley
as hard as she could; cranking harder couldn't make it go
any faster. Gunn bounced up and down in the saddle as if
urging her steel horse to giddy-up. Nell fancied that if Gunn

had a riding crop, she would have given it a try. Nell did her part to help by hunkering down, hunching her shoulders, and holding her chin level with the rim of the sidecar to make herself as aerodynamic as possible.

Gunn leaned forward, her determined jaw hovering just above the handlebars, and swung the whole contraption violently left. Nell's shoulder was thrown against the inside of the sidecar, but she kept her helmeted head from banging into the hot engine as she leaned into the turn. They had pulled onto a kind of road—not much more than a couple of neglected dirt ruts just wider than the Harley-Davidson and sidecar—that led from the tarmac through a few sparse, wind-twisted trees and into the Painted Hills ahead. A plume of dirt unfurled behind them, and Gunn wiggled the wheels a bit in an attempt to thicken the smokescreen.

Nell could hear sharp cracks and faint whizzing noises. She hoped they weren't bullets, but she could not in her haze of hangover and fear come up with anything else they could be. Gunn careened right and left and left and right. Leafy branches slapped Nell in the goggles and blades of grass snapped off and wedged themselves between her teeth. The road grew narrower still, and Nell ducked and shirked to keep from being decapitated by low limbs.

Nell could only hope that the woman in the saddle had any idea at all which direction they were headed. The road was a mere overgrown suggestion at this point; luckily the trees were sparse enough for their rig to drive around them. If Nell had been kicked out of her sidecar and told to walk back to the road, she'd have had less idea of where to begin than if she'd put her forehead on the butt end of a Louisville Slugger and spun around it a dozen times. The sensation in her drunken head and stomach was nearly the same.

After a few minutes, Gunn slowed the motorcycle and backed it into a crevice between two red and orange pillars of rock. Once they had tucked themselves in, Gunn killed the engine and cocked an ear to listen for their pursuer. It was silent. Not even a bird called in the clear blue sky above them. Gunn slumped in exhaustion, but she was grinning again.

Nell looked out of the slit where they were parked at the ridges of striped rock, the result of sediment being laid down and then carved away by wind and water. Across the path, where the sun shone brightly and nearly vertically into the little canyon, the rocks were bright orange and rusty red and creamy yellow. The rock walls next to her in the shade, though, were purple and blue with hints of green. She knew intellectually, thanks to her geology studies, that these were the same rocks here as the rocks a few yards away, but the light or lack of it made all the difference in their appearance. When she looked straight up, the purple rocks seemed to fade into the smooth blue sky, but the rocks in the sun stood in such contrast to the sky that there almost seemed to be a black line delineating earth from air.

"I think we lost him," Gunn whispered. "For one thing, he can't drive around some of the trees we did."

"If you'd asked me in advance, I wouldn't think we could drive around some of the trees we did," Nell said. "As it was, I was nearly beheaded by some of those low-hanging branches."

"You were not," Gunn scoffed. "Were you?"

"I ducked."

"I knew you'd be fine," Gunn said. She stood on the pegs and leaned forward over the handlebars to peek around the rock corner. "I don't see him, either. Let's push the bike a bit. It's quieter, and we used a lot of fuel in that little chase."

Nell hadn't even thought of the gasoline they were burning as they tore through the Painted Hills. She'd been too worried about the whiz-bang sounds coming from behind them for the first quarter-mile or so. "Gunn," she began, "was he shooting at us?"

Gunn put her boots on the ground on either side of the bike and started duck-walking it out while still in the saddle. "Push on the rock, Nell. I did too good a job of finding us a little crag to hide in, and neither of us can get away from this bike until we're out of it."

Nell put her palms on the rock and pushed. The friction scratched her palms; she hoped they wouldn't bleed. When they were clear of the rocks after a few seconds of grunting and shoving, she climbed from the sidecar and checked her hands. They were roughed up but not too badly hurt.

Gunn was another matter. Something had torn through her suit, shirt, and skin. A thin line of blood glowed between the white cotton and brown tweed like the red stripe of the rocks in the sun. Gunn twisted her neck and raised her left arm to examine the damage. "Yup, he was shooting at us."

"Gunn!" Nell was shocked. Her head was finally clear of its whiskey-induced haze. And then it was too clear. She had no idea what to do next.

"For someone who deals with dead people all day, you look pretty pale, Professor." Gunn opened her satchel and lifted the hem of the slip she had worn the night before.

She found a seam and pulled at it until it unraveled enough to tear off a length of fabric. "It's just a flesh wound, but I can't tie this up myself." She held the strip out to Nell, who took it.

Nell stepped closer to Gunn. "Do you need something to bite down on or anything?"

Gunn smirked. "What do you think is going on? I was grazed. It's a bad cut, nothing more, Florence Nighting-Nell. I'm not going to lose an arm, and you're not doing battlefield surgery. No bourbon or bullet-biting required." She set her jaw and looked forward, waiting for Nell to tie up her arm, which she held away from her body. "Though I wouldn't turn down a whiskey if somebody had a hip flask tucked away on their person." She looked hopefully at Nell.

Nell's stomach still threatened rebellion at the thought. "I'm really much better with the long dead than the freshly wounded," Nell said as she slipped the fabric between Gunn's body and arm.

"You need to tie it tighter. Tighter. Tighter. Nell! It's going to have to hurt me a little bit to make it tight enough to stop the blood while we bounce back to the road and race for the gas station in John Day. This has to last until we see Doc Hay." She reset her jaw and winced a bit when Nell pulled the knot as tight as she could. Gunn checked her arm, wiggled her fingers, and nodded. "That'll do. I can feel my fingers. Luckily," she lifted her gloved right hand, "this one works the throttle. The left only works the brakes."

The two women returned to pushing the motorcycle quietly down the road a bit, listening for the rumble of a car engine, the crack of a pistol, or the snap of a twig under the foot of the man in the black hat. Gunn would stop every once in a while, hold a finger to her lips, and cock her head as she listened, like a fox when it stops midstep and pivots its ears. Nell would freeze, every muscle rigid, afraid the sound of her galloping heart would ruin Gunn's aural acumen. Gunn would relax and say, "Nope," and the two women would go back to pushing the motorcycle along the twisting path.

Nell had the time to realize now exactly how very twisting and dangerous this path was. There were tire tracks on the outside edges of several sharp curves—tracks that could only belong to a Harley-Davidson with a sidecar. Above the tracks would be a scraggly fir clinging to the rocks with all the life force it could muster and a branch poking out with needles like a thousand tiny knives. Nell pulled her chin back and looked down at the goggles that rested at her clavicle. They were covered in tiny slashes of sap. She could have been blinded, if not beheaded. She felt faint. She leaned harder on her left hand, which rested on the rear of the motorcycle seat. As she half swooned, she caught sight of the white strip of fabric wrapped around Gunn's tweed bicep. Spots of blood bloomed like bachelor's buttons on its outside, but Gunn strode over the dirt and rocks as if it were a wedding aisle, back straight, eyes facing forward. Nell decided not to faint.

After a few minutes, the rocks moved away from the path and the scattered trees regained their sense of belonging and released their terrified grip on the striped rock faces. The road widened a bit here. There was only one dark stand of firs and scrubby shrubs between themselves at the entrance to the painted rock path and the paved road. Nell took this opportunity to find a second wind (or possibly a first, given the train wreck she'd been all morning) and pushed with more verve.

But Gunn stopped and swung a leg over the seat. "Better get in," she said, fastening her headgear on tightly. "We're not out of the woods yet."

"We're almost to the road. We must have lost him."

"He knows his car would never make it along the rotten road we took, and he knows we have to come out this same way. He also knows my gas tank is small and that the trails up here are tough on an engine. Those are the bad things," Gunn said, and Nell's second wind blew away, leaving her deflated. "But he didn't chase us on foot, which means he's tired, injured, or lazy. All of those are good things. Or he's patient, which is bad." Gunn reached behind her back and drew a small pistol from underneath her riding jacket. "That crafty coyote is going to be parked on the other side of that copse of trees," she said with a calculating gaze. She held the pistol out to Nell butt first. "We're going to fight fire with fire. You're the firepower, Professor."

Nell took the gun. She was a crack shot when it came to rifles and tin cans lined up along the fence, but this was an entirely different animal. "I can't kill anyone," she said. "I'm an archaeologist. I prefer my people already dead. No blood. Unless it's ancient and dried and possibly sacrificial."

"Kill someone!" Gunn snorted. "How much heat do you think that baby gun packs? The answer is, barely enough to pop this guy's Goodyears. Your job is to distract him from being able to aim his own gun too carefully. He's got a bigger engine, but it's hauling around a lot more steel than we are. Think light thoughts and aim to burst his rubber or spiderweb his windshield." Gunn cocked her knee to kick the motorcycle to life, then paused and looked into the sidecar. "Do you know how to shoot a gun?"

Nell shrugged without taking her eyes off the pistol. "Shotguns and rifles. I was pretty good with those." She held it out at arm's length, the way she'd seen it done in gangster movies.

"You'll figure it out, Professor," Gunn said. "Ready?"

Nell positioned her hands around the hilt, trigger finger poised. She nodded curtly, and Gunn stood on the clutch. They tore off into the trees with dirt and rocks skittering high into the air behind them. As they neared the copse, Nell rested her elbows on the sidecar for a bit of stability in case she really did have to shoot.

The car roared to life as they passed, just where Gunn said it would be. Nell could see the grimace on the face of the man in the black hat as he popped the clutch and lurched forward. He only made it a few feet before Nell fired. Her first and only bullet pierced his front passenger side tire. It deflated with a hiss and a growling, angry howl from the driver.

Nell blew the nonexistent smoke from the barrel and turned forward, her own self-satisfied smile matched only by Gunn's proud mug.

13

In Which Nell and Gunn Have a Breakdown

Gunn settled the engine at less than screaming eagle but more than Sunday drive in an attempt to use as little fuel as possible while escaping their likely pursuer over the hills. There weren't many people driving this road; the occasional truck full of cattle or wagon loaded with hay were the only vehicles they met as the road wound along next to a river at the bottom of a close canyon. After a few miles, the pavement ended, but a gravelly, unoiled, unfinished version of the highway continued.

Nell knew it wouldn't take long for the man in the black hat to change his tire. She should have shot two. She could have shot two. Certainly he didn't have two spare tires. She could have taken out his radiator. *Rats!* There was so much she could have done, but she had been so pleased with that one excellent shot. If only Gunn had slowed down a bit to let her take aim and disable the car completely. Nell twisted in her seat every few minutes to check for the black Pierce-Arrow and the black hat driving it like one of Satan's minions on a mission from hell.

The motorcycle gasped and rolled to a stop despite Gunn's standing in the stirrups and swearing like a logger at it.

"What's happening?" Nell called over the sputtering motorcycle and rider.

"Out of gas," Gunn said as she swung herself free of the Harley in disgust, nearly kicking Nell in the head in the process.

"You have got to be kidding me," Nell said with a panicked glance at the black oily road behind them. "How many times can this happen?"

"I wish I were kidding, sister. It's a one-gallon tank." Gunn squatted on her heels and threw her helmet and goggles down next to her in the dirt. She dropped her head into her gloved hands. "We're still probably ten miles from John Day." She looked up at the sky, then down at her shadow, then over at the bloody strip of fabric around her arm. "We'd better move if we're going to make it by dark."

"And before the man in the black hat changes his tire." Nell climbed from her sidecar, pistol in hand.

"Shit. Shit, shit, shit." Gunn stood and took her place to the left of the bike, palms on the handlebars. "You ready?"

"Where do I put this?" Nell held up the gun.

"Stick it in your waistband, at the small of your back, under your jacket but where you can get it if you need it." Gunn managed a quick look of admiration. "Nice shot, Nellie Oakley."

Nell nodded, tucked the gun in her dungarees, and took her place at the right rear of the bike, hands on the seat. They shoved. And shoved. And shoved. Every slight dip in the terrain was a moment to celebrate, no matter how fleeting. Helmets, goggles, and bags were jumbled in the sidecar. It became late afternoon, the hottest part of the day, and the sun hadn't reached anything like the western horizon, despite the fact that the horizon was crowded by the white-capped teeth of the Cascade Range. The hairs at the nape of Nell's neck became damp and curled, then soaking wet and flattened against her skin. Dust collected there like a clay shell. Nell noticed the sweat rolling off Gunn's neck with a small twinge of satisfaction. *So Gunn does sweat*, she thought, then realized it took pushing a motorcycle with a sidecar on an unfinished road in the afternoon sun of the Oregon high desert with a bullet wound in her arm to disturb Ms. Flagely's biological temperature regulation system.

The road meandered slowly along the river, up and down gentle slopes. It was the only possible route through the rocky canyon. On the downhills, the respite they got from pushing wasn't ever long enough to justify getting on the motorcycle themselves, so they'd just let go and catch up with the motorcycle at the bottom of the shallow trough, then recommence heaving the rig forward.

After about two hours of impersonating Sisyphus, the women spied a truck shimmering in the distance. Nell wondered if trucks could be oases, or if that term only applied to watery hallucinations. She and Gunn were resting in the shade of an outcropping of rock next to where the motorcycle had rolled to a stop at the bottom of a trough between two rises. She had been glad when Gunn flopped to the ground without a word, once she established that this was a rest stop, not that Gunn had lost so much blood she was collapsing.

Gunn's ears pricked up too, so Nell figured the truck couldn't be a hallucination. Gunn stood, brushed dirt from her pants, slicked half-melted paint from the tube in her pocket onto her lips, smiled her best smile, and waved her right arm in the air. Nell stood, brushed dirt from her dungarees, and peered suspiciously into the cabin of the truck. She didn't see any black hats, but she didn't see any particularly trustworthy faces, either.

Then a face she did know, one sporting a wide-brimmed straw hat, peered around the cab from where he was sitting in the open bed. Nell may not remember much from the night before, but she remembered that face. She clutched her satchel to her side, pressing the skull in its soft felt bag against her ribcage with her radius.

The truck slowed as it neared the motorcycle. Gunn waved and smiled; Nell didn't move an inch. Gunn's wave won them over, and the truck stopped. Casey and another cowboy of about the same age but with a permanent line between white back and tan neck at his shirt collar vaulted themselves out of the truck bed and onto the ground. The passenger cocked an elbow out the window, and the driver, an older cowboy with skin as striated and craggy as the Painted Hills, peered at the women.

"What on earth are you two ladies doing out here by yourselves?" the passenger demanded.

"Casey! Are we glad to see you!" Gunn said, ignoring the man in the cab. Nell didn't say a word.

"You know these gals?" the driver asked Casey.

"I thought I did," Casey said, "but I thought only one of 'em was the type to love 'em and leave 'em." He peered at Nell from under the brim of his hat with a twinkle of humor in his eyes.

Nell held her satchel to her sternum and looked up the road as if rescue trucks ran on a schedule as regular as the A Train and she'd wait for the next one. But Gunn had kicked the kickstand up out of the way and stood waiting for the word to wheel the bike into the back of the truck.

"You're the two wild women from the saloon last night," said the driver as he got out of the truck and came around to the Harley.

"I'm not wild," Nell said. "I'm a scientist."

"Wasn't that a blast?" exclaimed Gunn. She and the men positioned themselves around the rig at the back of the truck.

"Speaking of blast." The driver pointed at Gunn's arm. "Looks like you got grazed by, what, a .22? That is no wound for a woman."

"It's a scratch," Gunn said with a dismissive wave of her hand. "Everybody take a corner and lift. This old horse can take it."

"It's not a scratch, it's a bullet wound from the man who's chasing us," Nell finally said. "The man who is pursuing us as we speak. The man who only has to change one flat tire—I shot it—and come after us on what I assume is the only road around for miles. He must have figured it out by now. And we've run out of gas."

Casey lifted her sidecar into the truck while Gunn and the others hefted the bike. "Was it that guy from the saloon?"

"It was."

"Is that why you ran off this morning?" His voice was strained with the effort of lifting.

"It was."

"Well, that makes me feel less used." Casey's face was flushed, as was every face around the motorcycle. "You gonna help?" He squeezed the words through his vocal cords.

"Oh, yes! Sorry!" Nell ran to the rear of the bike next to Gunn. She planted her hands under the rear seat and heaved up and forward. Those hay bales had done her shoulders some good after all. The motorcycle landed in the truck with a bang and a creaking of suspension springs. The bed bounced a bit, but everything stayed put.

Gunn brushed her gloved hands together in satisfaction. "If you could just get us to John Day, we can fill up the tank, and I can stop in to see Doc Hay for some Chinese healing magic," Gunn said to the driver. "I don't think it's far."

"We're nearly there," the driver said. "But I don't like to leave you two on your own out here. Women should not be traveling alone on a motorcycle. Women shouldn't even know how to drive motorcycles. Those little electric cars, now, those were nice. Quiet, clean, couldn't go too fast or too far. Perfect for ladies."

"I don't see why any ladies shouldn't travel wherever they like, however they like," Gunn said as she hopped into the bed alongside the bike. "I like big engines and a saddle myself. John Day will do, sir."

He looked at Nell, offering her a chance to disagree, a chance to get a ride to civilization, a chance to not be shot at by men dressed like movie villains, a chance to be rescued like a princess in a storybook. Nell climbed into the truck. "John Day it is," she said.

The driver shook his head and shrugged, then got behind the wheel. Casey and Gunn sat on a plank bench near the cab, one on either side of the bike's front tire. The other cowboy sat on the wheel well by Gunn, leaving Nell to squeeze onto the other wheel well between the sidecar and Casey. She hugged the skull inside her satchel to strengthen her resolve.

"Why hasn't the man in the black hat come by yet?" Nell wondered aloud. "Did you men pass him on the road coming this way?"

"Haven't seen a soul," the cowboy near Gunn shouted as the truck's engine fired up and struggled back onto the road with its new heavy load.

"If he cut over to Monument, we wouldn't see him," Gunn yelled over the straining motor as it hauled its heavy load uphill. "Dammit, if we'd have gone that way, we would have been able to refill the tank and then lose him on the back roads on that side of the river. I was so flustered I just hightailed it straight on for Doc Hay."

"Who could blame you?" Casey shouted with sympathy. "It's what any woman would do."

Nell glared at Casey, and Gunn settled her amused gaze on him. "We are not any women," they said in unison.

"No, ma'am," said Casey and his cowboy friend.

14

In Which Nell Meets the Doctor in John Day

Gunn and Nell waved as the truck full of ranch hands pulled away from the filling station, its suspension bouncing happily now that it was free from the extra load. Casey waved his hat in the air as long as the truck was in sight. Then it crested a rise and disappeared around a wooded bend.

Gunn spun the gas cap from the tank and said, "Fill 'er up!" from her position in the saddle. The attendant stood mute and blinking, the nozzle in his hand, as his very small brain tried to figure out the most proper way to fill a motorcycle's gas tank while a woman was sitting astride it. He shuffled about, looking for the least offensive or suggestive angle, while Gunn tapped the sole of her lace-up boot on the clutch. He made a few attempts at moving the nozzle toward the hole, but he backed off immediately every time.

Gunn stopped his hesitant little dance by saying, "Do most women dismount from their motorcycles while you fuel them?"

"Yes, um, no, I mean, most women don't ride motorcycles."

"Do the men dismount?"

"Usually, yes, ma'am. If only to avoid any accidental spillage on their person."

"Well, now, that does make sense. My apologies." She stood on the peg and swung a leg over Nell's helmeted head to land neatly in a ballerina's fourth position near the rear wheel.

Nell climbed from the sidecar. "I don't want any accidental spillage," she said.

"Most women wouldn't," Gunn said. Nell couldn't suppress a loud and unwomanly guffaw that she attempted to hide behind the back of her hand.

The attendant finished filling the tank as soon as he could; if he could have made the gas flow faster, he would have. He accepted Gunn's coins as if they were hot enough to burn his palm and dropped them into a pocket of his coveralls.

Gunn remounted the Harley and kicked it to life while Nell hopped into the sidecar.

"You ladies shouldn't be—" yelled the attendant over the engine noise.

"Out here alone!" yelled Gunn and Nell for him. With a ferocious twist of the throttle, they were off.

Not that they were going far. A mere sixty seconds after giving it the gas, Gunn backed the bike off to a putter. There were a few buildings lining the road here, probably not even a dozen, Nell noted, but Gunn seemed to be looking for a left turn.

"Is this a town?" Nell yelled over the engine noise as they rolled slowly along the short main street. "I thought we were going to John Day to see a doctor. Or is John Day the doctor?" Why were so many towns out here given personal names?

"This is John Day," Gunn answered without meeting her eyes, "and more importantly, over there is Kam-Wah-Chung. Doc Hay can take care of this bullet wound there." She swung the bike off the main road. The motorcycle bounced along an unpaved stretch to a two-story house that still somehow managed to look squatty under the pine trees towering above it. It was nearly hidden in the deep shade, though it was the only building on the block, if the term block could be used for a grassy expanse dotted by giant firs and bounded by dirt roads. The first floor was constructed of hewn stone, while the upper half was timbered and painted deep green. Hinged metal shutters protected the windows from snow, sun, wind, thieves, prying eyes, and for all Nell knew the graces of civilization. Red letters over the door read "Kam-Wah-Chung." It was definitely not a hospital, and it didn't look like a doctor's office. It looked like a junk shop in Chinatown, the kind with counters full of curiosities and secret back rooms that Nell had never been invited to visit. Not that she put much store in superstitious Chinese quackery.

Gunn stopped the engine and made for the door. Nell stayed put, helmet and goggles in place. She didn't want to go into this shady building. She didn't want to stay in the sidecar. She didn't want anything at all from what sounded like a Methodist summer camp for boys or an offensively fashionable Orientalist speakeasy. She wanted to get Skully somewhere safe. She wanted to forget about Casey. She hugged the skull inside its black bag.

"Looks like a lot of mystic hooey in there," she said. "I'm not sure it's the kind of place you and I go for, Skully. They'll probably turn you upside down and pour some concoction of bird blood and tiger claw in you and call it an ancient healing potion. Nope, you and I are for the rigors of science, Skully. Not the swirling smoke of incense."

Gunn came to the door. "You coming in? They're making lunch, if you're hungry."

"I'm fine," Nell called. She released what had become a tight grip on the skull without her intending it.

"No you're not," Gunn said with her smirk. "Even Doc Hay knows that, and he hasn't even met you. Your aura is so foul it's penetrating the walls and ruining the medicines. Come have lunch."

"I'm not hungry."

"You are hungry. And hot. And hungover. It's making you cranky. Come inside." Gunn waited in the doorway, but Nell didn't make a move. "They've got geodes."

"Geodes?"

"A lot of them. Thunder eggs, they're called in Oregon. They're everywhere out here. Doc's patients bring them as little presents, or sometimes as payment." Nell didn't leave her sidecar, but she did glance at the house a few times, so Gunn added, "And they have some unidentified bones."

"Bones?" Nell sat up. "Are they human? Do they even know? They should not be taking bones from the ground on their own. They should have contacted the authorities, in case there was foul play, or the university so they could be properly removed and cataloged and studied."

"These bones have been in this house longer than anthropology has been taught in universities," Gunn said.

Those were the magic words, far more magic than "please" could ever be. Nell unstrapped her headgear, stuffed the skull inside her satchel, and walked toward the building.

Gunn swung herself out of the way as if she were the door. "Welcome to Kam-Wah-Chung, Golden Flower of Prosperity."

Nell felt as if she'd stepped into one of the new dimensions proposed by physicists, one where the interior of a building could be far larger and hold far more than you could ever imagine by looking at its exterior. This was more than a secret room in the back of a shop. The whole house was filled with boxes and bottles and jars stacked on shelves from floor to ceiling, and it was full of scents and smells for which Nell had no reference at all. She didn't even know if she was smelling animal, vegetable, or mineral. Most likely, the tang in the air with a hint of sweetness and sweat was a combination of all three, and possibly some Chinese elements like essence of wood and water. There were bones of a not too distant vintage—mostly animal, Nell noted—on the shelves and tables. There were also S-shaped serpents trapped forever in canning jars and desiccated turtles that were destined to spend eternity on their backs, their shiny patterned bellies on offer.

Nell leaned back outside the door to check the length of the wall. It was about thirty feet from corner to corner. She stood straight in the doorway. The room she was in was on its own more than half that size, and there were doors on both interior walls and a staircase leading upward. She leaned out again, and back in. Must be that feng shui the Orientalists in New York were always raving about.

"Miss Flagely!" A thin man, taller than Nell but not Gunn, emerged from another room in the maze of what must have been thousands of rooms in this little house tucked under the trees. He wore a small black hat above his friendly eyes and had sharp cheekbones. He spoke with a thick accent, though his welcome of Gunn was unmistakable.

Gunn approached him and made a small bow, which he returned. "Doc Hay, this is Nell Kelly."

Nell bowed as Gunn had. "Nice to meet you."

"A scientific young lady," said a second man who entered the room from another of the infinite rooms. He was younger than Doc Hay, with a rounder face and crisper English. He walked toward Nell with his hand extended. "Lung On. You can call me Leon."

Nell shook his hand. "Hello, Leon. I am Nell, and I am indeed a scientist. Specifically, I am an archaeologist. I study human remains. Bones."

"Ah! Bones. Fascinating."

Doc Hay spoke in urgent Chinese, and Leon listened. They were looking at Gunn's silk-wrapped arm. "Doc says you need immediate care," Leon said gravely. "You must have an herbal compress and fresh bandages, or you will lose the arm to infection within the month."

Nell made a disapproving little sound. That was the way with these traditional practitioners: make it sound far more terrible than it is so that when their hokum worked on what was actually but a scratch, you'd be back for more and ready to throw cash directly into the till.

Gunn unwrapped the hem of her slip from her bicep, and Doc Hay stepped closer to examine the wound. "It's just a scratch," Gunn said dismissively to Leon, who translated for Doc Hay. Nell nodded in agreement with Gunn.

"Doc says indeed, it is just a scratch," Leon said after the old man had spoken again in Chinese. "But if you don't keep it from becoming infected, just a scratch will become just a case of gangrene."

Doc loosely wrapped his long fingers around Gunn's arm and drew her through one of the doorways. Leon extended an arm inviting Nell to follow, and then he brought up the rear. The house was a maze of tiny rooms, closets jammed with jars filled with powders, liquids, animal bits, and unidentifiable substances. There were entire shelves of split geodes, their rough gray shells surrounding layers of lavender crystals with a hollow center. Some of the jars' contents seemed to glow through their glass containers, and some seemed to sparkle. The occasional floating eyeball followed Nell's movement as she passed through the rooms. A shiver traveled down her unwilling spine. *Stop it, Professor Kelly,* she admonished herself.

They came to an examination room. Its walls were white in a nod to modern hospitals, but it was as crowded with strange substances as the rest of this rabbit hole of a house. Doc Hay sat at a low table and slid a mortar and pestle toward himself. He poked in the cabinets for powders, which he weighed on a golden balance scale and deposited in precise amounts into the mortar.

"Doc Hay is one of the most respected and visited doctors out here," Leon said to Nell, "among all races of people."

"Even Caucasian people? Cowboys and ranchers?"

"Even Caucasian people," Leon smiled. "Doc Hay has earned quite a reputation in the decades we have been living in John Day for healing the sick and wounded. Many of his ingredients are the same as those used in a hospital, but many others are ancient Chinese medicines. You know Professor Martingale at the University of Oregon?"

"I've met him," Nell said, "but how do you know him?"

"He studies medicinal plants, and he has been a great help to Doc Hay. Many of the plants we were importing from China have family members here in Oregon that are much cheaper to use and perform the same functions."

"Ethnobotany," Nell said. "Professor Martingale's field is called ethnobotany." She allowed herself to take a modicum of interest in the hokum.

Gunn had removed her jacket and blouse and now stood in her silk camisole and tweed trousers, her blood-crusted arm bare. Doc Hay used a cold cloth to wipe it clean and bamboo tweezers to pick out little bits of debris. Gunn inhaled through her teeth, then exhaled slowly. Doc Hay nodded, then smeared the thick, smelly paste onto a clean piece of linen. He placed it on the slash in Gunn's arm, and she gritted her teeth and drew in a breath.

"It burns like ice," Gunn said.

Doc Hay needed no translation; he'd certainly heard that complaint every time he used this compound. "Good for you," he said with a smile and an encouraging nod. He carefully wound wrappings around her arm and pinned them. He started speaking in Chinese, and Leon translated.

"The formula is one of the most famous in Chinese medicine called *Yunnan Paiyao*, or 'white medicine from Yunnan province,' which was officially invented in 1902 but has actually been in use a lot longer than that. It uses *Chuan Shan Long*, or the dragon that penetrates the mountain, and borneol, which in Chinese translates as 'ice slice,' thus the cold feeling. Only one man in all of China who knows the whole formula; the rest of us do our best with what we have put together." Doc Hay chuckled, and Leon continued for him. "*San Qi*, known here as notoginseng, makes up about 70 percent of the formula and can be used on its own for wounds like Gunn's, but it's much more powerful if you mix it with the other ingredients."

Gunn yawned and seemed near to passing out from boredom. Nell found Doc Hay's explanation via Leon very enlightening and far more precise than she'd expected. Maybe these men weren't old kooks in the woods after all.

"You need to keep that clean," Leon explained to Gunn, "and change the outer bandages every day. The compress can stay on for two days, then you rip it off." He made a violent motion with his hand. Nell flinched, Gunn did not. "It may bleed a little, but probably not. Keep it covered at least a week, and come back here if it turns red, seeps pus, or a dark line travels up your arm and across your shoulder, toward your heart."

The idea of any one of these things happening was enough to make Nell feel woozy, but Gunn nodded, her red lips set in a grim line. "Got it, Doc," she said to the old man, who grinned and patted her on the back with his small, soft hand. Then he took some of the powder he had applied to Gunn's arm from the mortar and mixed it with honey in a small bowl until it made a firm, sticky pill. This he rolled in red powder and wrapped in a small square of waxed paper. He presented it to Gunn, and Leon explained that she could take the pill the next day to take trauma out of the heart.

Doc Hay said one word, and Leon translated: "Lunch." The doctor led the women through the labyrinth again, and Nell was sure this was an entirely different set of rooms they crossed through. There seemed to be more little rooms serving as connected storage closets stocked with crates of medical or general store goods than as actual, proper household rooms.

At the sound of a tinkling bell, Leon requested that they indulge a quick detour. Nell was afraid to leave the group as it trouped through Kam-Wah-Chung; she wished she'd thought to leave a trail of breadcrumbs, if she had breadcrumbs. Gunn was right; Nell was hungry. The bell turned out to be the little brass ringer above the general store door. Two loggers with beards and sweaty flannels waited at the counter.

"Gunn!" exclaimed one of the men as she entered the room behind Leon. When Nell entered after Gunn, she thought she recognized the men from the store in McKenzie Pass two days before. It seemed like two decades. "What are you doing here?"

"Doc Hay fixed up a little scratch in my arm," Gunn said, offering her bandaged bicep as evidence. "What are you doing out here?"

"Loading up on supplies for the new show," replied the logger, "and Doc and Leon have the best prices on the most goods between Eugene and Boise. We're making our way over to a stand in Idaho. What are the chances we'd meet up again? You staying in John Day overnight? You got a place to stay? We've got a room just down the road."

"I'm sorry," Nell interjected, "but we've had a very trying twenty-four hours, and Miss Flagely really should rest."

The loggers looked disappointed. Gunn opened her mouth to set them straight on her health and availability that evening, but Leon jumped in first. "Nell is right. Gunn should rest." Nell was feeling more confident about these Kam-Wah-Chung men every minute.

Gunn quit her protest when Leon agreed with Nell's inexpert medical opinion. She tilted her head at the disappointed loggers and shrugged.

"Can I help you gentlemen?" Leon said, and the loggers presented him with a list of supplies to be fetched.

Nell wandered about the room while Leon poked about in the labyrinth of rooms, ferrying out crates of coffee, tobacco, soap, iodine, Campbell's soup, and Quaker oats. She found carvings of each animal in the Chinese zodiac, wooden snuff boxes with inlaid lotus designs, and carved jade pendants perfect for sending home to wives and girlfriends.

One of the flunkies toted crates to the bed of their truck while the other paid the bill from a roll of cash from his pocket. He removed the rubber band that held it together and placed one bill at a time on the counter until he'd reached the amount rung up on the cash register. Leon placed the bills in the till and thanked the men, who tipped imaginary hats at Gunn and Nell on their way out the door.

"I don't know why we couldn't go with them," Gunn said as she sashayed from her corner to lean on the counter—on her right elbow. "We could have quiet fun. Not like Nell is used to, with her whiskey and her cowboys and evil men in black hats following her around. Nice, quiet fun with a couple of lovely loggers."

"I would like nothing more than some nice, quiet fun," Nell said with a frost that dropped the temperature of the foyer ten degrees, "but someone insists that we ride around on a motorcycle while a man shoots at us."

"I don't know what you're complaining about. I'm the one with a wounded wing. A Kelly-style belt of whiskey would do me some good. Lift my spirits."

"Alcohol will do you no good, Gunn," Leon said with a wag of his finger. "It will thin the blood and make it flow faster, more freely."

"No," agreed Doc Hay with a nod and a smile. "One hundred harmonies."

15

In Which Nell Finds Dope Fiends and Animal Friends

If the exterior dimensions of Kam-Wah-Chung corresponded to the interior, Nell figured they should be in Idaho by now. She followed Gunn and Doc Hay (Leon brought up the rear) through several more rooms, one of which was set up with pristine bunk beds with tucked-in white sheets, an infirmary for cowboys, loggers, gold miners, and railroad workers. For every room of powders and tinctures and glass jars of dehydrated animal parts there was a room stocked floor to ceiling with general store merchandise. There were tins of coffee great and small, crates of tobacco and soap, newspapers and magazines from Portland, Pendleton, and Spokane—even a few from Back East, like Chicago and New York. The eastern issues were out of date, but not by more than a week.

They at last came to a sitting room that seemed like it belonged to a private residence. It had two matching overstuffed chesterfields upholstered in low-pile gray velvet facing a coffee table whose polished wooden top was perched on the heads of four carved wooden dragons. Doc Hay tucked himself into the corner of the sofa nearest the door, and Nell sat opposite him. "Did Leon and Gunn get lost?" Nell asked when they didn't bring up the rear.

"No," Doc Hay shook his head. "Leon bring tea, help Gunn's pain." Nell noticed that his excellent posture made him seem taller when he was sitting than he actually was when he was standing.

Leon came in with a tea tray that had a drab brown clay pot in the center and four small, translucent white porcelain cups without handles arranged around it. He placed the tray on the low table and went to a sideboard to retrieve napkins and small, round cookies on a plate. Nell took a steaming cup of tea from the tray. She held it in both hands, closed her eyes, and inhaled. It smelled like green plants and white flowers, with a heady undertone like a secret garden. She sipped and found it delicious, if bitter, as if she were drinking all the parts of a forbidden plant. She opened her eyes and looked to Leon.

"*Bai He Di Huang Tang*," Leon explained. "One hundred harmonies and fresh rehmannia, a fuzzy, trumpet-shaped flower." He brought his fingertips and thumb together in illustration.

"It's lovely," Nell said, taking another long sip. She didn't want to be rude and mention that Leon might have steeped the tea a bit long and brought out the bitterness of the plant.

Gunn leaned on the cushy armrest and curled her boots onto the couch next to her, which Nell thought was rude, though it did look comfortable. She kept her own brogues on the floor, her knees touching. Gunn had a dreamy, content look on her face, which also looked nice, and which Nell also considered inconsiderate. Gunn seemed to be receding from the room, which was a poor way to treat one's hosts. Nell kept her hands on her cup and her spine as erect and proper as possible, though she felt like receding too. Just a little. Just for a bit.

"And a light tincture of opium," Gunn said.

"What?" Nell's eyes flew open and turned their gray lights on Gunn, whose eyes were closed, her long black eyelashes resting on her cheeks like feathers. She would be no help. Nell looked into her cup, which was already half empty. She couldn't believe she'd liked it. She had even thought of asking for seconds.

"Gunn," said Leon with a disapproving frown.

"Not in yours, of course," Gunn said. "But I needed just a tiny bit, for the pain, and Nell could certainly use a little unwinding. It was just there on the shelf as we passed by. And then it was in my hand while we were in the kitchen. And, miraculously, a bit was dropped into my teacup and Nell's."

"What did you use?" Leon held out a hand, and Gunn placed a small brown glass bottle in his palm as if she were a child caught with contraband.

Leon examined the label, which was written in small, crisp Chinese characters. "Luckily, you picked a very weak tincture to pilfer from our shelves." He slipped it into a hidden pocket and looked at Nell with beatific reassurance. "You will be fine, Nell Kelly. You will likely only feel relaxed, as Gunn guessed without knowing what she was doing."

Nell felt reassured when Doc Hay nodded in agreement. She sat back against the cushions and steeled herself for the relaxation.

"Unless you're prone to hallucinations," Leon said as he sipped his tea. "But you don't strike me as the hallucinatory type."

What if I am the hallucinatory type? Nell thought. *What if I never snap out of it? What if I become a drug fiend? What if I never get a chance to slap the lipstick off Gunn's face for doing this to me?* Her heart began to beat, not quickly, but so hard she could see it through her thin jersey shirt. She began to take inventory of her vital signs.

"It's a very weak tincture," Leon said. "A medicinal dose for pain and anxiety, not a dose that would do anything for the men who smoke in the dens. Don't worry, Miss Kelly. You won't become a dope fiend from this tea."

"Let it flow through you," Gunn said without opening her eyes. She grinned and continued receding from the room, physically now, until all Nell could see was her red-lipped smile. "It's tea, after all. It's going to flow through you whether you like it or not."

Nell did not like it, but there wasn't anything she could do but wait it out and retain control of herself. She leaned back into the sofa cushion. "I'll be fine," she said. "I'll be fine."

Now Doc Hay and Leon faded from their seats on the opposite sofa, leaving only the matte gray velvet behind. Nell sat alone in the room holding the fine porcelain teacup with her sun-freckled hand. She hadn't been sun freckled since she was a teenager spending summers on the farm. She pushed her brown leather sleeve up and saw the contrast between her exposed wrist and her shielded forearm. Everything above the bony pisiform was milk white with the occasional tiny brown circle. She wished she had a pen to connect the dots. Maybe there was a message hidden there from her body to her mind. She let the leather fall back into place and noticed how it blended with her newly tanned skin. The hide of the jacket became her hide. "I'll be fine," she said softly.

She had to admit, she did feel pretty good, if a bit floaty. And she was grateful for the break from Gunn. There was no unringing the opium bell, but she trusted her intellect. She would keep her wits about her while the others faded right out of the room. She was a scientist. She had a pencil and a notebook in her satchel; she could record the experience and return to the data when she was sober. Her satchel was very far away, though, on the floor, which was at least a dozen feet from the seat of the sofa. She was going to have to stretch her arms past their physical limits if she wanted to reach it. It would be a tough task to accomplish without spilling what was left of her tea. She looked at the tea cup, the satchel, the tea cup, the satchel. *In for one, in for all,* she thought and downed the rest of the tea, including the floaty bits at the bottom. She took a deep breath and extended both arms, the left hand to set the cup on the tray on the coffee table and the right to grasp the strap of her satchel. She leaned back and returned her arms to their normal lengths.

She drew out her notebook, flipped to a fresh page, and wrote in careful print: "Stretched arms to 12 ft. (approx.), replaced tea cup, retrieved satchel. Do not expect lasting effects from arm stretching; will report in 24 hrs. Consumed full dose (what was dose? ask Leon for Rx) of opium so as not to spill during cup replacement."

Nell looked at her note, satisfied with its precision and the shape of her handwriting. She'd always had lovely penmanship; everyone said so. She began carefully shaping the alphabet, uppercase and lower, as she had in grade school, which made her giggle a little.

She heard a soft sound and looked up to find a gray wolf with golden eyes padding into the carpeted room. "Hello, wolf," she said. "I suppose it was too much to expect that I wouldn't experience a hallucination after ingesting opium. An hallucination? A hallucination." She noted: "Wolf has entered room" and held her pencil poised to record the conversation she assumed was coming.

"Hello, Professor Kelly," said the wolf. He licked his lips as if she looked delicious.

"You know my name! You seem to exist outside my imagination, but you can speak, which points very strongly to your being a figment of said imagination," Nell said, noting these observations under the headings "Real" and "Imaginary." She scrutinized the wolf. "You do look familiar. Are you imaginary?" *Might as well come right out with it,* she thought.

"We've met," he said. "And we'll meet again. You have something of mine, and I aim to get it back."

"I don't think so." Nell looked at her satchel. She had so little. Nothing she couldn't carry in a satchel in a sidecar.

"Don't play dumb, Professor Kelly. You may be a woman, but you're no dumb bird."

"Hey! Watch it!" said a magpie as it flew in the window and perched on the wolf's back. The wolf seemed annoyed, but he did not shake the bird off or snap at him. "Some birds are quite intelligent. That's how we survive in a world full of wolves. We pay the wolves to bring us things we want." He cocked his head and eyed the round lump in Nell's satchel. "And we pay handsomely for things we want very badly, don't we, Wolfie?"

"The skull?" Nell followed his gaze. "That's not yours. Neither of yours. It belongs to science. Besides, you're imaginary animals. You don't have thumbs to hold it, or corporeality, for that matter. It cannot belong to you." She held up her notes, which did indeed have more entries in the "Imaginary" column, including the fact that the magpie had no pockets for the money he said he had.

"Actually, it's mine," said a smaller, dun-colored canid who appeared in doorway. "I defeated the monster and flung him to the four winds. The blood of the monster that I washed from my paws remained near the Snake River and became the Nez Perce. I am their Father. They would like me to come home. Surely an anthropologist like yourself can understand."

Nell snorted. "I'm an archaeologist. Your little story might work on a cultural anthropologist, Coyote, but not me. That's not how evolution works."

"Evolution!" said the magpie with a flutter of his wings. "We're on the same team there, Professor Kelly. We've got to keep this specimen out of the hands of both the super-stitious Indians and the biblical literalists. The difference between us, Professor Kelly, is that I have the money to back up my beliefs."

A rattlesnake slithered into the room between the wolf's legs, making everyone nervous, animal and human alike. He raised his head a few inches and coiled his body beneath him just in front of the wolf's feet. "I would move heaven and earth to have that skull."

"You don't belong here," Nell admonished. "You're a timber rattlesnake from Back East, the only kind of pit viper I've ever seen." She noted this under "Imaginary."

"He wants it to smash it," squawked the magpie, flapping his wings at the snake, who gave a warning rattle and hiss. "I'll keep it safe. I'll admire it. I'll love it. I'll show it to my friends."

"Your belief in science is being pitted against a tribe, a religion, and a pile of money," said the wolf. "Are you so sure that your precious lab coat can protect you?"

"I am." She wondered if the white of her lab coat would meld with the usual white of her skin like this leather jacket did with her suntanned skin. The thought made her feel a bit safer in the presence of the rattlesnake, no matter how hallucinatory he might be. She noted the experiment's premise in her notebook for later testing.

"Suit yourself, Professor Kelly. We'll meet again very soon." The wolf turned and loped out of the room, with the coyote, bird, and snake following.

Nell took the time to record the conversation as well as she could, noting that the rattlesnake was of the wrong species for this region and that the magpie seemed not to like him. The coyote was quite reasonable, but she wasn't giving anything to a figment. An ermine scampered into the room and onto the opposite arm of the couch. It was a cute little thing, much prettier than the other animals who'd visited. It was creamy white with a black tail and an odd black patch on top of its head between its ears.

"You've got your winter fur," Nell said curiously.

"Nell!" cried the ermine. "Did you see that wolf?"

"Yes," Nell said, wondering how all these creatures knew her name. "We had a conversation, he and the magpie and the coyote and the snake and I. I took notes."

"You talked to him?"

"Yes. He told me that I'm not the only one who wants the skull. But it hardly matters, because I've got it."

"You do indeed," the ermine said. The sleek furry body transformed before Nell's eyes into Gunn, her legs again curled under her on the sofa cushion. "I don't know about the bird and all the rest, but that wolf was the man in the black hat."

Nell placed a sympathetic hand on Gunn's leg. "Gunn. Dear girl. That was an opium-induced hallucination." She pointed to the chart in her notebook.

"It was," agreed Gunn, "and I would know more than you. But don't discount a hallucination if it tells you true things."

"*An* hallucination." Nell was not sure this was correct, but it was the opposite of what Gunn said, which was sometimes the more important point.

Leon and Doc Hay materialized on the opposite sofa. Leon said, "Your heart may be trying to tell your head something it doesn't want to hear."

"You were an ermine," Nell said to Gunn.

"I was?" Gunn was pleased.

"How can you be happy to be a weasel?"

"I bet I was cute."

"You were cute," Nell admitted.

"How did you transform?" Leon asked Nell. "What animal form did you take?"

"I was me," Nell said.

"No you weren't," Gunn said. "You were a bobcat kitten. Your eyes were that same innocent yet potentially deadly gray."

"You weren't here," Nell said to Gunn. "I was not a kitten. I took notes." She held up her pad. "Kittens cannot take notes, nor can they converse with wolves, magpies, and snakes. Though the wolf did look a bit hungry when he saw me." The looks on Leon's and Doc Hay's faces said she might not be handling the opium as well as she thought.

"Let me see those," Gunn said and snatched the pad from Nell's hand. "Hey, you did take notes. Good ones. I expected opium-addled gibberish, or maybe little cat tracks. But this is a transcription of your conversation with a wolf, a magpie, a coyote, and a rattlesnake, which you note was of a non-native species. It makes a surprising amount of sense. And you started an alphabet sampler."

"Lab notes are crucial in any new or experimental situation," Nell said. "And I have excellent handwriting."

Gunn handed the pad back to Nell. "It looks like you've got some pretty big forces, including money and religion, lined up against you. And a lone wolf. That's the dangerous kind. Unpredictable."

"He's not a wolf," Nell said as if Gunn were a willful child playing a game of pretend. "He's a man. This creature who came in here and spoke to me is an hallucination. A hallucination." Now they both sounded wrong.

"I guess you are susceptible to hallucinations after all." Leon leaned forward and peered at Nell with eyes that turned golden. His nose grew to a sharp snout, and pointy russet ears grew on either side of his small black cap.

"Now, don't you go turning into a fox, or whatever you're supposed to be," Nell said. "And you," she looked at Doc Hay, "put those rabbit ears away. I've had just about enough."

"Fair enough," laughed a very human Leon. Doc Hay gave his pink nose a last twitch and returned to humanity himself. "There are cold ham and cucumber sandwiches in the kitchen icebox whenever you're ready to eat," Leon said.

"I should start looking for those sandwiches now," Nell said as she stood up. "By the time I find whichever room might be the kitchen with the icebox, I'll be starved."

Gunn stood and thanked the men for their hospitality then followed Nell as she made her way through endless corridors. After each turn taken, Gunn would say "hotter" or "colder" over Nell's shoulder. Finally Nell turned around and in exasperation said, "If you know where the kitchen is, just take me there!"

"I don't know where it is," Gunn said. "I thought we were playing a game."

"You're not playing it right," Nell accused.

"Sure I am. While you look for something, I say hotter or colder."

"You're supposed to say hotter when I'm close to the target and colder when I'm moving away from it, not just at random."

"Okay," Gunn said.

"Did you ever play this game when you were a kid?"

"I saw other kids playing it."

"But you didn't play it?"

"My friends were all grown-ups," Gunn said with a shrug of her uninjured right shoulder. "I played with bones and sherds and little hand-carved canoes that the natives gave

Daddy. I was the anthropologist's daughter on digs and the weirdo with skulls on her shelves in our neighborhood. My pets were taxidermied. But I studied their games the way Daddy studied the Umatilla people. I filled whole notebooks with taxonomies and rules and gender associations when I was a girl."

Nell felt equally sorry and exasperated. "Who would have thought that your lack of childhood friends would get us lost in a Chinese medicine shop at the edge of the American West." She laughed once. "Who would have thought I'd even be in a Chinese medicine shop at the edge of the American West?"

"We're not lost," Gunn said, "and where would you rather be?"

"The lab."

"You lie."

"I do not."

"You love it out here."

"I am enduring it for the sake of significant anthropological discovery."

Gunn sidled up to Nell. "You like it. You like me. You like," she leaned in close to Nell's ear and whispered, "the sidecar."

Nell crossed her arms, took a deep interest in a nearby jar of sparkling green powder, and said, "I don't mind it."

Gunn nodded resolutely and wrapped her right arm in the crook of Nell's left. "Let's find those sandwiches. We'll get a snack, sober up, and head over to the hotel down the street."

"That is a plan I approve of," Nell said. "I am hungry now, and I'd love to get a real night's rest."

Gunn looked at Nell from the corners of her kohl-rimmed eyes and said, "There's a little informal speakeasy…"

"Alone," Nell clarified, "and sober."

"Of course," Gunn conceded as they walked the narrow hallways. "Unless we see Casey."

"Alone, Gunn."

"Right."

16
In Which Nell Is Betrayed in the Boondocks

The next morning, Gunn and Nell were happily tooling along astride or inside the Harley in the hazy sunshine of eastern Oregon, out where they only had to share the landscape with cattle and the purple mountains' majesty of the Alps-like Wallowa Mountains ahead. Nell could glimpse their snowy caps occasionally as they twisted through the deep-green pines and alders that lined the road, which was once again paved. She tilted her helmeted head back to face the sun, which was already high in the sky, despite it only being midmorning. Above her, Gunn's red mouth was moving, snarling when it wasn't forming words Nell couldn't hear, and her eyebrows were crinkled in a scowl above her goggles. Nell watched, her gaze as hazy as the sky, as Gunn snarled, glanced in the rearview mirror and recommended spitting angry, unheard words. Her right wrist twisted harder on the throttle, but the Harley was giving all it could give already.

Nell twisted in her seat. The big black car was behind them again, and the man in the black hat was at the wheel. Nell wished she knew as many curse words as Gunn seemed to know, given the stream of insults and frustration that seemed to flow without pause from the motorcycle's driver. Nell was surprised to find she wasn't so much afraid this time as annoyed. *Just go away already,* she thought. *I caught the skull fair and square. You lose, flapjack.* She fumbled at her waistband to grab the pistol.

Gunn swung the Harley off the paved road and onto an oiled dirt road that led into the woods, throwing Nell against the side of the sidecar before she could pull out her gun. The man in the black hat didn't have nearly enough warning to slow down and slough the heavy Pierce-Arrow around to follow them. He pressed on the brakes hard—too hard—and skidded out of control. He released the brakes long enough to get the wheels rolling against the pavement with purpose, but he was too far past to catch up with the nimble motorcycle. Nell found in her heart the tiniest inkling of gratitude for the quick little motorcycle and sidecar, gratitude that was wiped out when they bounced over a tree root and she nearly bit her tongue in half on the return to earth.

Again Gunn steered this way and that on ever-smaller roads, much like she had done in the Painted Hills on the western side of John Day. Nell kept an ear cocked for the roar of the car's engine, but heard nothing over the clamor of their own little engine. She cocked her other ear for sounds of gunfire and held the little pistol at the ready. She wished she knew how to check the chamber; there should be four bullets left. One for each tire, if she was careful. Or maybe two through the radiator.

Ahead, the trees cleared and a couple of small buildings huddled together against the harshness of nature. It was a bright, sunny morning, but these little houses and businesses seemed to have spent too many winters crushed by heavy snow to stand up straight and appreciate the summer when it finally came. The homes were nearly identical and lined up as if for inspection; they had to be company housing for workers of some kind. There was a general store, a gas station, and a train station, probably for shipping out whatever it was the workers were building, or mining, or cutting down. Something nearby was making a grinding, clanging racket in any case.

There were strange piles of gravel snaking in long twists of stone rope just past the center of town and a loud chugging sound echoing in the shallow valley. Gunn piloted the bike toward the sound, which became an unbearable din as they neared a stranded paddle boat. No, not a paddle boat, Nell realized, but she didn't have a name for such a strange contraption. It sat in a few feet of murky water, which was being churned beneath the boat's shallow hull. A conveyer belt as wide as her shoulders that hauled up giant metal buckets full of rocks extended above and below the two-story wooden boat's central line, and a few men scampered about on the decks tending to the noisy machinery. A man sat in what would be the pilot's house, if there were anywhere to pilot the boat, but the pond it sat in was barely bigger than the boat's own footprint. The snakes of gravel seemed to be following the boat as it crawled forward more slowly than Nell could walk.

Gunn pulled the motorcycle into a thicket nearby, dismounted, and hailed the men on the boat with a wide wave of her arm. Gunn had pulled in so close to the bushes that Nell had to climb over the nose of the sidecar to get out. *Typical*, Nell thought as she removed her helmet and goggles.

"Welcome to the Sumpter Dredge," Gunn said to Nell at the top of her voice. "No one ever comes out here; it's noisy and ugly and uncivilized. We can hide here for a bit. I worked here with Daddy after I quit secondary school. He'd come pick through the tailings for old bones and arrowheads, and I'd help him catalog what little he found. It was awful."

"What are they dredging for?" Nell yelled, forgetting for a minute about their pursuer.

"Gold!" Gunn said.

Nell tucked the pistol into her helmet with her goggles and put them in the nose of the sidecar, which was hidden from the road by the shrubbery, then slung her satchel with the skull across her chest. Gunn hung her helmet and goggles from the handlebar, and the two women walked toward the makeshift, moveable gangplank to board the noisy contraption.

The dredge was slowly snaking its way around Sumpter, scooping the bottom of the valley up, sifting out the gold, and leaving the gravel tailings behind itself. Nell wondered how long they could go on before the valley was chewed up and spit out the back of this dredge, and how much gold they could sift from the gravel.

The men stopped their ant-like activities long enough to come to the boat's railing and wave at Gunn. She pointed to herself and Nell then gestured toward the deck where the men stood. They nodded exaggeratedly and waved the women over. Nell and Gunn crossed to the deck, and Gunn shook hands with a handsome young man in coveralls. His hair had probably started the day slicked back neatly as any city sheik's but was already falling free of its place against his scalp. He leaned in to kiss Gunn's cheek then pointed up. Speaking would be pointless in the din of the machinery as it pulled earth and water up by the bucket load and dumped it into a bin to be sifted. Gunn nodded and grabbed Nell's hand to lead her up a narrow wooden staircase in the center of the boat.

It was slightly quieter in the pilot house of the boat; there were fabric baffles and batting arranged against the walls and in all the corners. "It's a little better up here," the young man said in a voice strained from primarily being used to shout, "but not much. Captain, you remember Gunn Flagely." He carefully and fully shut the wooden door behind them, damping the noise a bit further.

"Of course." The captain shook Gunn's hand with a leer not at all hidden by the scruffy brown beard and mustache crawling across his cheeks and down his neck.

"And this is my fellow anthropologist Nell Kelly," Gunn said, and the captain took Nell's extended hand as well. He gave her a lesser leer, but it was a leer nonetheless. "We're in a bit of a bind, Captain. It's a long story, but we've got a bad man in a black hat driving a big car on our tail, and we need to hide out for a bit."

Gunn made herself comfortable on a wooden bench that ran along the back of the pilot house. Nell attempted to do the same, but she was unable to find the same gracious ease that Gunn could summon no matter where she was. Bed of nails, red hot coals, pilot house of a gold dredge— Gunn could sit and smile and look as if she were on a velvet divan. Nell could feel every knot in the painted board, plus a splinter that threatened to breach the seat of her denim trousers. And then there was the brain-silencing clamor of the dredge as it crawled like a ravenous, angry turtle in a pond of its own making. Nell needed a plan, but it was impossible to think one up over the sounds of the dredge doing its gold-digging job.

Nell gave up on appearing at ease and stood next to the pilot as he worked. It was not a frenzied job, as the dredge moved inches at a time and the likelihood of a storm blowing in and flipping the dredge keel-side up in its shallow personal pond was beyond remote. "Does this thing have a keel?" Nell said loudly next to the captain's ear.

"No, ma'am. Hardly needs one."

Nell nodded. "How fast does it move?"

"She's a real goer. We manage seven yards a minute, and about twenty buckets."

"So you dredge up the earth and sift out the gold?"

"Yes, ma'am." The pilot gave Nell a look she'd seen many times before and had learned to ignore, the look that said she was asking more questions than a lady should. But he continued, "Each bucket gets sifted, sorted, and dumped over those riffles you saw down there to let the gold drop to the bottom where we can get at it."

"How many men work on the dredge?"

She got the look again, but she waited impassively for the pilot to answer. "It only takes three men to work the actual machinery. The rest of us are here for maintenance and managing. That's me, the manager, and the pilot, though there isn't much piloting to be done. The boys just call me Captain for the hell of it."

"Do you sleep on board?"

The captain gave up on the look and resigned himself to prompt answers. This Nell had also seen before. "Oh, no. That would be pure hell. The machinery never sleeps, so we got a couple guys who do night watch while the rest of us cross that gangplank back to solid ground and sleep in bunks. It's like a logging camp, sorta."

"That is quite interesting," Nell said.

"Yup," said the captain, unsure how to respond.

In truth, Nell had run out of interest, and therefore out of questions. She returned to the bench next to Gunn.

"How long are we going to hide out here?" Nell said in Gunn's ear.

"A while, I suppose," Gunn answered. "The man in the black hat will never guess we're here. We'll just let him ride on by, then we'll slip into his slipstream and head for Daddy's dig."

It wasn't much of a plan, but Nell couldn't think of a better one in this noise. The bench was no more comfortable now than it had been twenty minutes before, so she again rose, this time to look out the window toward the town of Sumpter.

"You may want to rethink that plan," Nell shouted to Gunn. "He's already here."

"What?" Gunn leaped to her feet and looked out the window. The big car was skidding to a dusty stop near where Gunn had hidden the Harley. The man in the black hat emerged from the driver's seat and peered at the pilot house from under the brim of his hat. The pilot held out his hand with his thumb turned up. The man in the black hat returned the gesture and loped toward the gangplank.

Nell and Gunn turned toward the pilot with mouths agape.

"Sorry, ladies," the pilot shrugged. "Call came through from the dredge's owner this morning. If we were to see you, we were to hold you. He says you stole something from that fella down there."

"He stole it from me first!" Nell cried.

Gunn lunged for the door, only to find it locked. The man who had led them to the pilot house stepped in front of the door's window and wagged his finger at her.

"Anybody on duty today's gonna get a big bonus," the pilot said.

"I'll bonus you," Gunn said as she stalked toward the pilot. "Nell, show him we mean business."

Nell slung her satchel across her body and stalked toward the man. She tried to match Gunn's jutting chin and menacing stare.

Gunn looked at her. "I mean, show him the pistol."

Nell whispered from the side of her mouth, "I left it in the sidecar."

"What?" Gunn said, half in disbelief and half because of the noise.

"I left it in the sidecar," Nell repeated louder. "I thought we were with your friends."

"Oh, for God's sake," Gunn said. She started to pace the pilot house, but it was only a couple of boot strides wide. Her pacing only caused her to roar in further frustration.

"It can't be that bad, can it, Gunn Flagely?" asked a familiar gravelly voice. Nell wondered how she could hear it over the sound of the rocks. "After all, I'm going to take away all of your troubles right now. As soon as Nell Kelly gives me the skull."

Nell turned from the pilot to the open door. The man in the black hat filled the doorway, though he had to tip his head forward a bit to make his hat fit inside the frame. His yellow-toothed grin and stubbled jaw were all she could see of his face, but the muzzle of his pistol was quite plainly visible as it was pointed at her. Again.

"Never!" Nell said. She clutched the satchel to her chest.

"Stay back," Gunn said, stepping in front of Nell. "I'm not afraid of you."

"And I'm not afraid of you," said the man in the black hat. He stood toe to toe with Gunn. It seemed to Nell even the machinery was waiting for someone to make a move.

It was Gunn who moved. Her left hand shot forward and pushed the pistol back toward the man's shoulder. Then she grabbed it by the barrel, wrested it free from his surprised grip, and tossed the gun into her right palm. She held the barrel under his chin. "How about now?" she purred.

"Still no," he growled, taking a matching pistol from his rear waistband, the very place, Nell noted, that Gunn had told her to keep her pistol. She grabbed at her back, just in case she was more prepared than she remembered, but it wasn't there.

The man moved a pace away from Gunn. He held the pistol at arm's length and aimed at her head. He moved along the wall toward Nell, who stood inanimate with fear. He grasped the strap of her satchel and yanked hard. Nothing happened. He twisted it around his hand and yanked again, but still nothing happened.

"Nell here is no willow-limbed flapper, and that's a well-made British leather satchel, mister," Gunn said. "You're not going to break either one that easily."

"What I can't break, I'll take," grumbled the man. He lifted Nell onto his shoulder like a sack of horse feed, never taking the gun from Gunn's forehead.

"If you take her, you take me too." Gunn lowered the pistol and stepped so close to the man their noses nearly touched.

The man let out one dry desert of a laugh. "I don't want one woman; you think I want two? I'm only taking this one," he jostled Nell on his shoulder, "because what's in her skull makes that old skull valuable. Nobody's going to pay top dollar for a monkey skull, and the owner of this rig says she's the one who's got the say-so." He backed out of the pilot house without lowering his pistol lest Gunn should leap onto his other shoulder. He ducked and twisted a bit to fit Nell through the doorway without banging her up too badly, a courtesy Nell begrudgingly appreciated.

The man in the black hat turned and ran as best he could down the stairs and across the gangplank, Nell grunting with each bouncing step. She held her head up to watch Gunn come to her rescue. Gunn started to run after them, but the man with the greasy hair held her arms in his meaty paws. He squeezed her bandaged left bicep a little more than necessary, and she winced.

"You haven't heard the last of Gunn Flagely!" she yelled as the two crossed the gangplank.

"Careful! Careful!" Nell called to her captor, but he didn't slow as they boinged across the wooden boards. "It's not me—it's the skull! It's fragile!" That got his attention. He slowed his pace once they were on firm ground. "However old this skull is, it's not going to last long if you bounce it around like that. Then neither of us get what we want."

He didn't put Nell down, but he did walk smoothly to the car. He returned his pistol to his waistband, opened the rear-hinged passenger side door, and dumped Nell into the back seat. He retrieved the pistol before closing the door and held it leveled at her forehead as he walked around the long hood and entered on the driver's side.

"What do you want with me?" Nell said as coolly as she could, which was not as cool as she wished.

"What I want, Professor Kelly," he said as he turned the key, "is to sell that skull for a shitload of money." He mashed the gas and spun the car onto the road out of Sumpter.

17

In Which Nell Learns of Lewis

Nell crossed her arms and fumed in the back seat of the Pierce-Arrow, which was quite spacious. She turned her furious gaze on the back of the man in the black hat's head, hoping to burn a hole through the matted gray mess that was his hair and stop his scheming brain with the heat of her anger. It did not seem to be working.

She wanted to ask questions: Did he have a name? Where were they going? How long had it taken him to put his scheme together? When had he learned she was coming to the University of Oregon? Was there a ransom? How much was she worth? How much was the skull worth? But she refused to give him the satisfaction of her curiosity. She preferred the silent fuming. He allowed it.

A half hour passed before Nell was moved to speak. "I'm hungry," she said.

The man in the black hat did not answer.

"Hey!" Nell sat up in the back seat and placed her head near the driver's shoulder. "I said I was hungry."

"I heard you," he answered in his low voice. Its pitch nearly matched the roar of the engine; no matter how loudly he talked, he would never be heard clearly. He might have answered her the first time. It was nearly as noisy in here as it was in the sidecar. Or more likely, Nell thought, that sidecar had caused permanent damage to her ossicles. She'd never hear properly again.

"What about it, then? Can I at least get lunch on this excursion?" Nell had never been kidnapped before. She had no idea it would make her so mad.

"This isn't a school field trip," said the man with a cruel curl of his lip. Nell moved back a few inches in case he felt like biting. The man was filthy, with beady eyes and prickly cheeks; biting did not seem out of the question. Maybe her opium dream hadn't been so far off.

"What is it, then? A tour? A private conveyance?"

"A kidnapping."

"That is so ordinary," Nell said, doing her best bored flapper impression. She rolled her eyes in a way worthy of Gunn and threw herself back against the tufted upholstery of the rear seat. She crossed her arms again and gave up any notion of mercy. There was a town up ahead, she could see, and a sign that welcomed them to Baker City.

The man pulled the car to the curb in front of the tallest building on Main Street, a three-story hotel with a tower on the corner. Gold paint on the doors said this was the Geiser Grand Hotel. He stopped the engine and twisted to look at Nell with cold, gray eyes over a long, straight nose. "I need to place a telephone call to my first potential buyer, the guy who put me onto you in the first place. The rich guy who owns the dredge and has a thing for *antiquities*. That means old, fancy shit that old, fancy people will pay big money to own."

"I know what it means."

"You will come inside with me and tell this man that the skull is very, very old and worth a crate of cash. If you behave, you may order a picnic lunch to eat in the car on our way to the rendezvous. If you do not behave, I will shoot out your left kneecap. Are we clear?"

"Sure," she said with an insubordinate flick of her eyes. "And it's called a patella."

"I don't care." He exited the car and pulled Nell from the back seat with his fist clenched near her elbow like a steel vise. Nell gripped the black sack with the skull inside with equal fervor. She looked up and down Main Street for a flapperish fiend on a motorcycle barreling down on the town in a cloud of dust, but she saw only a few folks walking along the sidewalks and a couple of cars tootling slowly along.

"She's not going to save you," said the man in the black hat as he shoved Nell through the door.

"You obviously don't know Gunn Flagely," Nell retorted.

"I know her and her kind better than you do," sneered the man as he steered her across the quiet lobby toward the front desk, where a man with blond hair and round, silver glasses waited for them without looking directly at them. "She'll turn her front wheel toward the first handsome man with a bottle of whiskey she comes across and forget all about you. She won't even remember your name by tomorrow morning."

"That's not true."

"Isn't it? She's been a steadfast friend since you've known her? Never gotten you in trouble? Always sober and respectable? Not likely to drop everything and take off on a whim with a stranger in her sidecar?"

"Like you're an improvement in the morals department." She was being pretty reckless, she knew, since her kidnapper had a pistol. She had nothing but irritation.

They stepped up to the front desk, where they finally became the business of the blond man, and so he acknowledged them with a nod. The man in the black hat put on what he probably considered a charming smile. "My girl here and I need to see Mr. Thompson."

The concierge smiled slightly and pressed a button on the switchboard. He held a receiver to his ear and kept his gaze trained on the man in the black hat. There was a squawk in the receiver, and the concierge said, "A man in a black hat is here to see you, along with…a woman."

"Professor Nell Kelly," Nell chimed in, claiming the title fully.

The concierge did not relay this information. The squawk of an answer was short, and he replaced the receiver. "He's in the suite. Up these stairs," he gestured at the wide staircase, "and his room is at the far end." He gestured to a spot over his head on the second floor.

Nell tipped her head back and admired the large stained-glass window that flooded the lobby with bright colored light. The man in the black hat steered her across the floor and up the stairs, where she had to pay attention to her feet again.

They walked past a few doors to other rooms before reaching the single door in the far wall. The man in the black hat raised his knuckles to knock, but the door was opened by a trim man with neat brown hair and a crisp white shirt buttoned to the throat under his black vest. "Lewis. So good to see you."

"Only if you've got the money," snarled the man in the black hat as he dragged Nell into the room. The neat man closed the door softly behind them.

"I've always got the money," he said as he followed them into the sitting room. There were two large leather chesterfields, but no one sat down. He took up a spot by the window, and Lewis, as she now knew him, halted her just inside the room.

"And this must be Professor Kelly," the buyer said. "You are…unexpected."

"You expected a man," Nell said.

"I did, I'll admit. You can call me Mr. Thompson."

Nell stared at him. She would not be calling him anything. They always assumed a professor was a man.

"I'm here about our friend Coyote," said the man in the black hat. He looked meaningfully at the bag dangling from Nell's hand.

"We call him Skully," Nell said.

"Lucky for me, he was in the hands of Professor Kelly when I found him. She can tell us right now what this thing is worth. Unlucky for me," he threw a glare Nell's way, "Professor Kelly is a girl and friends with Gunn Flagely. That has made things more difficult. My rate for antiquities acquisition has gone up accordingly." Nell noted that Lewis's vocabulary, when it came to making money, was much more sophisticated.

Mr. Thompson froze. His face contorted as if a diseased bird had dropped out of the sky and died at his feet. "Gunn Flagely." His disgust was all-encompassing.

"I got the professor," ventured Lewis. "Who cares what some girl on a motorcycle does?"

"I care. Everyone cares. That, Lewis, is the problem. Anything with Gunn Flagely's fingerprints on it becomes news. Big news. This skull was already a known entity within academic circles; attaching Gunn Flagely's notoriety to it will not help the situation. Last week, a few no-name eggheads in stuffy rooms cared where this thing was. Soon, everyone who has a passing acquaintance with literacy will know that Gunn Flagely is on the case. Fees for 'antiquities acquisition'—a phrase you've recently added to your repertoire, Lewis—do not go up when the acquisition involves Gunn Flagely. They go down. To zero." The timbre of his voice had also dropped to zero.

"But I got the professor," Lewis repeated. "I brought her and the skull all the way across the state, just like you wanted. She's the one who can verify it, even if she is a girl. I did what you asked. I get the fee."

"All the way across the state with Gunn Flagely on your tail?"

Lewis rubbed the back of his neck. This was going so badly Lewis might have to just let Nell go, she figured, which brightened her day a bit. Or shoot her, which was not such a brightening thought.

"If Gunn Flagely has any part in this, I am no longer interested," said Mr. Thompson. "It's too hot; the lid will blow and the G-men will be all over me. I have business to attend to. I am a pillar of the community. The deal is off."

"Gunn Flagely is not a problem," Lewis assured Thompson—and likely himself.

"Gunn Flagely is always a problem," said Thompson and Nell at the same time.

"Everyone knows that," Nell added with a shrug.

Lewis exhaled every molecule of breath from his lungs. The muscles in his neck and jaw became taut cables. Nell doubted very much that she would get her promised picnic lunch no matter how she behaved.

"So you're reneging on our deal," Lewis said.

"I'm surprised a lowlife like you knows the word renege," said Thompson, as calm and cool as a mountain lake.

"I know it because rich bastards like you keep doing it to me," snarled Lewis. "You aren't the only asshole in the West with piles of money and a hankering for old, fancy shit."

"Antiquities," said Thompson.

"You hear about those monkey trials up there in Spokane? Those religious types will pay far more than forty pieces of silver for something like this. This is your last chance."

"I don't need last chances, or even second chances. I, as you say, am a rich bastard. Best of luck." He turned around to gaze out the window, his hands clasped behind his back. Lewis and Nell were very much dismissed.

Nell turned and walked toward the door. The man in the black hat followed her, which surprised her, but really, where else could he go?

As they descended the staircase under the stained glass ceiling, Nell said, "That sounded like it went well, Lewis."

"That bastard is only one in a long list of potential buyers," grumbled the man in the black hat.

"Will the others care that Gunn Flagely is on your tail? And probably her father, and the University of Oregon?"

"None of those sound like the law or bounty hunters to me, and those are the only pursuers worth running from."

"Sounds like Thompson didn't agree."

"Rich men are cowards. Money makes them soft."

"Aren't you worried you'll become cowardly and soft when you sell Skully for a pile of money? I could save you the career-ending embarrassment of becoming a soft thief by hitching the next ride out of here with my black sack of troubles. We'll be out of your hair, and you can continue on your hard, broke, manly way."

"No, I am not worried about becoming soft," said Lewis, leaning close to Nell's face. He pinched her arm in his vise-like grip and marched through the lobby.

"Don't I get lunch?" Nell asked as she was strong-armed into the back seat of Lewis's car. "You promised."

"No."

18

In Which Nell Escapes!

Another silent hour passed in the Pierce-Arrow. Neither Nell nor the man in the black hat—Lewis, she now knew—said a word, and no buzzing Harley-Davidson appeared in the large rear window. Nell sank further into the back seat. Nell had spent days in a motorcycle sidecar and now half a day in a much faster sedan, and still she hadn't reached the end of this godforsaken state.

Nell sat up as the car slowed on its way into a small town—La Grande, according to the sign. Nell thought the name was more than a bit optimistic. The buildings huddled together along the main street like horses standing shoulder to shoulder against the wind. Hills rolled away from the town toward the snowcapped mountains to the east.

They had barely left La Grande when they found themselves entering—and immediately leaving—the little town of Island City. From here the road tilted sharply upward, and the engine heaved its way into the Wallowa Mountains. The road twisted low along the river and climbed high to hug the side of the hills. Nell kept to the left side of the car, both to keep herself from the temptation to look down over the side of the cliff they were driving along and to keep a bit more weight on the inside track. She stroked the skull inside its bag with her thumb as if it were a worry stone. The outside tires would sometimes catch a bit of gravel on the narrow shoulder of the road and send it flying down into the valley below.

The man in the black hat did not apparently share her concern. Nell had to trust that he knew these roads well. Otherwise, with the speed he was coaxing out of the engine even on the ascents and the way he wheeled around the corners, she would have to assume he was trying to kill them both. He had to want to live himself, she figured, which meant as long as she was in the car with him, she was safe. It sounded preposterous even in her own mind.

Nell was feeling a bit green around the gills when they finally pulled into a gas station in a little town called Enterprise. The tank in this car was far bigger than the one-gallon teardrop on the Harley, but Lewis was burning through the gasoline by driving fast up and down these high mountains. Lewis exited the car and signaled to the attendant, who shambled from his little wooden shack across the dirt to the pair of pumps. The man in the black hat shut his door and leaned against it, arms and ankles crossed as he chatted as near to amiably with the attendant as he could manage with a hostage in his back seat.

Nell, the hostage, kept her head low so the attendant wouldn't notice her. She slid quietly across the bench seat and placed her hand on the handle to open the far door. She kept her focus on Lewis's back. She slowly pressed on the lever and unlatched the door without opening it while the attendant was talking. Neither man turned toward her. She clutched the black bag and made a break for it.

She heard the angry shout of Lewis and the perplexed shout of the attendant, and then the pop of Lewis's pistol. The bullet hit wide and low, sending a puff of dirt into the air to her right. He was aiming for her knees. She figured the best way to prevent them from being shot was to keep them moving, so she ran.

Not far from the gas station was a handful of buildings that served as a town along a run of dirt that served as a main street. She could see the wooden porch and swinging hinged sign that told her there was a general store to aim for. She ran, knees pumping, as Lewis followed at a fast lope, bullets pinging the ground around her. *How many bullets does the man have?* she wondered. Her leather jacket flapped against her back as her shoes pounded the ground.

She skidded right, the heel of her brogue sending a cloud of dust flying into the air, and leaped onto the boards of the porch and grabbed at the door handle. It didn't budge. The latch didn't flip, and the lights were out. Locked. She pulled and pulled and pulled. Finally, she turned around.

Lewis had caught up with her. He stood in the street, pistol aimed casually at her patellae. "You still hungry?" he asked.

"Yes," Nell said. She looked up and down the street, which was empty. No people, no cars, no motorcycles, and no open businesses. *It's Sunday,* she realized. *Goddamn it.*

"Well, if you mosey on back to the car like a good girl, they'll feed you when we get to our next potential buyer. They're always eating up there. But if you don't mosey like a good girl, I will shoot your kneecap and carry you to the car. Then the good people of Paradise will have to do their best to bandage you up and keep you from bleeding out rather than feeding you. And they are better cooks than doctors. They don't go in much for medicine."

Nell heard an engine far in the distance. It was a loud, rumbling sound, with a bit of a clatter. A sound like a Harley-Davidson with an empty sidecar. All she had to do was buy herself some time and get that pistol pointed elsewhere. There was only one way to do it. It was a bluff, but it might work. It was the kind of bluff no one ever called. She hated to use feminine tricks on anyone, even bad guys like Lewis, but she had to make a move, and this was all she had.

"I'm not just hungry," Nell said with an evasive glance down the street. "I need...supplies."

"Supplies?" Lewis started. "What kind of supplies could you possibly need?"

Nell dropped her womanly bomb. "I'm menstruating."

Lewis's vocabulary didn't seem to include the reproductive cycle as he merely cocked his head and said, "Huh?"

"My menstrual period? My time of the month?"

Lewis was getting it now. His knees buckled a bit, and he drew back further beneath his black hat.

Nell used her hands to gesture at her pelvic area. "I'm bleeding from my—"

"Aaaargh!" Lewis clapped his hands to his ears. "I got it! For Chrissakes, shut up! Aargh!" He did a little uncomfortable turn in the street.

Nell could hear the engine getting louder, but it still wasn't in sight. But now the pistol was off her; Lewis was waving it around as if to shoot her words right out of the air.

She fired another volley. "I need Kotex. Menstrual pads."

"Aargh!" yelled Lewis again. He couldn't hear the approaching motorcycle over his own discomfort and exasperation.

At last a plume of dust arose to the north. It was now or never. Nell clutched the black bag and ran for it.

Turned out to be never. Lewis was disgusted, but he wasn't slow. He stuck out a pointy-toed boot as Nell ran past, and she flew headlong into the dirt. She skidded to a stop and felt the cold blunt end of the pistol at her medulla. She was smart, she was strong, but she had never been a graceful girl.

"You will get up and get to the car now. And fast." Lewis's gaze flicked toward the noise of the Harley's engine.

Nell made it to her knees with the pistol never leaving her skull, then slowly stood. Lewis grabbed her elbow in his familiar iron grip and quickly marched her to the car. He threw her in the back seat and started the car before he'd even climbed all the way in himself. He popped the clutch and stomped on the gas so hard he rose from his seat. The car roared past the incoming motorcycle. Through the cloud of dust between them, Nell could see Gunn's angry eyes behind her goggles and her red-painted lips form a grimace as menacing as anything Lewis had in his repertoire. Nell put her hands on the rear glass and watched Gunn attempt and fail to spin the motorcycle a hundred and eighty degrees; the empty sidecar made the turn impossible, and the engine stalled out. Gunn leaped from her saddle and ran after the car, screaming obscenities for as long as Nell could see her.

Lewis used the brake to turn the car abruptly right onto a side road that, according to a sign at the corner, led to Paradise. Gunn was gone.

19

In Which Nell Is Not Welcome in Paradise

Nell was on her own, rescue-wise. The road the man in the black hat was driving down became less and less civilized, and they hadn't exactly started in a metropolis. She set her chin on her fist and her mind on the problem.

"Are you going to kill me, Lewis?" she asked.

He turned his head toward her but not his eyes, which remained fixed on the road. "Depends on you, Professor Kelly," he said out of the side of his mouth. "If you behave yourself, I don't see why I'd waste the bullet."

"Am I valuable, in a ransom sense?"

He perked up a bit, his gold eyes shining in the mirror. "Are you?"

"You're the criminal; don't you know the value of everything and everyone?"

He nodded. "Your parents rich?"

"Nope. Farmers."

"Brothers? Uncles? Dowager aunts with inheritances to bestow?"

"No. Sorry."

"You're not valuable in almost any sense." He settled back into his seat and followed the twisting road with his gaze again.

"But you're still not going to kill me."

"You keep talking, woman, it gets more likely."

Nell sat back too and watched the sun set over the tops of the Douglas firs. A bad guy in a sadly stereotypical black hat was not going to keep Nell Kelly—scratch that, Professor Kelly—scratch that, Sidecar Kelly—down. Anyway, no two-bit movie villain was going to send Sidecar Kelly back to the farm, her tail between her legs.

But Lewis didn't want to kill her. She held this thought in her mind and turned it over in the late afternoon sunlight like a specimen to study. He could have kidnapped Dr. Flagely, she supposed, though she had to admit she was probably an easier target. A sitting duck, helpfully sitting in an office with the skull in her outstretched hand. Dr. Flagely was, after all, at a dig site surrounded by his admiring students. But Lewis recognized her as the expert, as Professor Kelly, as the one who could prove the age and therefore worth of this skull. She felt a bit proud at being worth kidnapping, if not worth ransoming or using even a single bullet to kill her.

The man in the black hat drove into the darkening night. The huge headlights mounted at the far reaches of the long hood illuminated surprisingly little of the narrow, rocky road. The trees along the sides of the road loomed black and pointed against the deep-purple sky. Every star was out, and the Milky Way was scattered across the sky as if someone had spilled a box of diamond dust. It was lovely, Nell thought, even though she was seeing it from the back of her kidnapper's car.

It was some time later when Lewis finally said, "Welcome to Paradise." The headlamps were the only lights—no shops, no houses, no gas stations were lit up at this hour. She could see a couple of darkened farmhouses ahead, their residents asleep with the sunset the better to arise with the sunrise and tend to the animals in the barely discernible barns out back and the cattle that were likely further afield. The big car's engine and its tires throwing pebbles from the rutted dirt road were the only sounds.

"No hotels in Paradise," the man in the black hat said quietly as he pulled into a long driveway. Grass grew as high as the curved fenders between hard, dry dirt tracks. The trees along the drive gave way to a clearing with a big, two-story house, a couple of smaller shack-like houses, and a huge barn with a gaping black maw where the door should be. Lewis crept the car into the maw and cut the engine. Dim starlight leaked through cracks and knots in the barn walls. "I'll be sleeping in that hay," he pointed to a fluffy pile stacked against the left wall. "Whether you choose another pile of hay or the back seat of this car is up to you. Mind you, I am a light sleeper, and my friend Colt wakes up at the slightest noise." He patted his right hip.

"You said you wouldn't kill me," Nell said. "Besides, you need me if you want to get any real money for your trouble."

"I need your brain and your ability to convey whatever's in it that's actually useful. Your kneecap does not enter the picture."

"You keep threatening my patellae. I'm starting to think it's a fetish with you." Nell pondered her choices through the car's windows. "I'm sleeping in here," she said, stretching out along what she thought of as her back seat. "And I'm locking the doors."

"Fine by me," said the man in the black hat. He reached back and snatched the bag with the skull inside from where it rested next to her, exited the car, and shut the door behind him. Then he backed to the hay pile, his eyes never leaving the car, flopped backward, settled the skull on his steel cable of a torso, and tilted his hat over his face. Before settling all the way into sleep, he patted his right hip again, knowing Nell was watching him and his bony charge from the car window.

Hours later, Nell awoke in a sweat. Not the cold sweat of panic at having been kidnapped, but the hot sweat of morning sun shining through the open barn door and into the back seat of the Pierce-Arrow. She had taken off her jacket to use as a pillow, but it was like an upholstered greenhouse in there. Her cheek stuck against the brown leather as she sat up, leaving an imprint of the seam on her cheek. She clambered into front seat, opened the car door, and gulped air like a fish who's been thrown back by a fisherman gulps water.

"Morning," said Lewis. He was standing near the rear bumper and had been up at least long enough to settle his hat on his steel-colored hair and brush the hay from his black trousers. The black bag dangled from his fist. "There'll be breakfast inside." He nodded toward the farmhouse.

Nell wanted to refuse the food and drink of her enemy, like the Count of Monte Cristo, but her empty stomach chose that moment to proclaim its own wishes in the silence of the barn. She climbed from the car without a word and slung her jacket over her shoulder, one finger hooked in the collar, with the nonchalance she'd learned from Gunn. Her stomach growled again, ruining the effect.

Nell sauntered toward the house. She could hear the holster hit the man in the black hat's hip as he walked close behind her: *whap…whap*. As she neared the house, she slowed, unsure if she was headed for the porch, the side door, or some other entry. The man in the black hat passed her, bounded over all four wooden porch stairs, and held open the screen door with a flourish of his hand. "After you."

Nell gave him what she hoped was a withering look, as she hadn't had much practice at withering looks and could only do her best. They entered a large kitchen with a wooden floor worn smooth and a long table lined with benches. Every seat at the table was taken by men in dungarees and shirts neatly buttoned all the way to their Adam's apples, despite the warmth in the dry air even this early in the morning. Nell didn't know the exact time, but the sun was hanging low over the mountains to the east, and these men looked like they were fueling up for a long day. A phalanx of women in pleated bonnets and old-fashioned ankle-length calico cotton dresses brought plates of pancakes and eggs and bowls of oatmeal to the table, then cleaned away the dirty dishes as the men plowed through the meal. The men finished up in silence and filed out past Nell and Lewis, who waited near the door. The women removed the dirty plates, then sank into the vacated seats and helped themselves to the food left behind on the platters they had earlier lined up along the center of the table.

The man in the black hat led Nell to the far end of the table and guided her again with his hand clenched around her elbow to an empty spot on a bench. All the men but one, who was too old and paunchy to work the fields or ride the fences or beat the swords into ploughshares or do whatever it was these people did, had left the table. He sat at the far end with one hand on either side of his nearly empty plate and took in Nell with small, gleaming black eyes that hovered over his wild gray beard. Nell wondered if her fate might be worse than being kidnapped, worse even than death: maybe she had been brought here to marry one of the men. Maybe this was how Lewis was going to get some fast cash while he waited for the dredge owner to pony up, by selling her into white slavery. She swallowed her panic, which brought on another rumble from her stomach. One of the women, who was probably Nell's age, stood, wiped her hands on her apron, and brought Nell a clean plate and fork from the dish drainer by the sink. She gave Nell's denims and brogues a cold once-over before turning away with a shake of her head. Nell speared a cold, rubbery pancake from the nearest platter and scraped a little pile of bright-yellow scrambled eggs onto her plate.

"Excuse me," Nell said to the room at large. A half dozen faces turned toward her. Apparently they hadn't expected their guest—or anyone, least of all a woman—to speak. "I'd love a cup of coffee." She smiled her winningest, toothiest smile. No one returned her smile, nor did they move to fulfill their guest's request. Nell's smile fell. "I can get it myself, if you just tell me where the pot is."

"We do not drink coffee here," said the man. His voice was as even as his black-eyed gaze was steady. "We do have fresh milk."

"That would be lovely, thank you." *What kind of crazy farm is this?* Nell wondered. *Are we so far out in the wilderness that there's no coffee? Paradise. Hardly.*

One of the women, a younger one barely out of her teens, placed a chipped clay cup full of creamy white milk next to Nell's plate. The pancakes were terrible, the eggs were bland, and the milk was warm, but she downed it all and speared the last pancake on the tray for herself. At least the deep-purple, berry-flavored jam for smearing on the pancakes was delicious.

As Nell finished her breakfast, the women cleared every plate but hers and washed every dish at the sink. They never said a word, and they never met Nell's eyes. Now that she noticed, they avoided looking up at anyone. They might steal glances at each other behind their bonnets, but they averted their eyes near Lewis and the pudgy man even more than they avoided Nell. When the kitchen was as close to sparkling as a mostly wooden décor could achieve, except for Nell's dishes- and crumb-strewn corner of the table, the women scattered to the four winds. They were like wraiths in embroidered aprons. Wraiths who liked to cook and clean and do needlework and churn butter in silence.

Then it was only Nell, Lewis, and this old wild-bearded man at the head of the table. The old man raised his hands toward the ceiling and spoke in ringing, pastoral tones. "Praise God for bringing us Lewis, who has in turn brought us evidence of Satan's trickery on earth and the wicked daughter of Eve who can confirm this most terrible falsehood, which is turning our nation's youth away from the one true path and toward wickedness. In Jesus's name we pray." He opened an eye and turned it on Lewis. "Care to remove your hat, Lewis?"

"I do not," grumbled Lewis. He leaned an elbow on the table and waited for the old man to finish.

Nell stared at the old man as if he were insane. "Who are you people, and what have you done with the year 1926?"

He brought his gaze down from the heavens to Nell. "Thanks to you and your kind—those serpents in the trees like Darwin and Scopes and the hell-raiser Clarence Darrow and all the rest of the nonbelievers—the people of this earth are doomed to burn in hell. They see these old skulls and old bones and dinosaur tracks left in rocks and they believe what Satan's scientists tell them. They believe these things to be millions of years old. They believe in so-called facts rather than the Word of God, and they will burn in hell for their sin. I believe in a world created from darkness by God, with man and beast created by God, as laid out in Genesis chapter one. Seven days, not seven million years." He chuckled at the very idea.

"If you think so little of me and that skull," Nell gestured at the bone in the black bag that sat on the table between herself and the man in the black hat, "why the hell am I out here in the middle of nowhere eating your pancakes? Which are terrible, by the way. You should pray for a better recipe." She had never been so rude to anyone in her life, but this guy was getting on her last nerve.

"We are rich in spirit as well as rich in Mammon's dollars, thanks be to the Almighty and his generous followers with their regular tithes. You tell me that skull is a real-deal million-year-old human head," said the man, wagging a finger in the bag's direction, "the oldest in the land, and I'll destroy it like you want to destroy the souls of schoolchildren. You tell me it's a fake, like that missing link they paraded around at the monkey trial last summer, and I'll hold it up like Moses held the tablets, for all the world to see, and I will tell them one of Satan's best hath told me of his trickery. They will drop their false idols of skeletons and rocks and come back into Jesus's fold, in his name we pray, amen."

"Well, that doesn't even make sense," Nell said with a skeptically cocked eyebrow. "The Bible has brought hope and comfort to untold numbers of people, my own family included, but it doesn't say a word about dinosaurs or the age of the earth or anything."

"Oh, but it does tell us the age of the earth. Mathematicians from your numbers-worshipping tribe have calculated the age of the earth to be six thousand years, according to the Holy Bible. God left us the clues right there in the good book to figure it out for ourselves."

"But you don't think the fossil record or ancient skeletons might be clues God left for us to figure out?"

"These are false revelations planted by Satan to lead mankind astray."

"So no matter what I say, you win."

"No matter what you say, God wins."

"Good Lord." Nell rolled her eyes.

"Yes, indeed." The old man tented his fingertips together.

"That's not what I meant."

"I know."

"Fine," Nell said in a huff. She removed the skull from the bag and looked Lewis dead in the eye. "If you want me to look at the skull with my tribe's scientific and satanic eye, I need Dr. Flagely's notes and photographs of the dig site. For lo, they are the scriptures of my people, and without them I cannot draweth a scientific conclusion."

"Surely you can make an educated guess," said Lewis, full of snarling menace.

"I do not like guessing."

"Take your best guess," Lewis leaned across the table and hissed, "and I will take you back to Gunn Flagely."

"Gunn Flagely!" roared the pastor. "How dare you utter the name of Jezebel in my home! That fallen daughter of the first sinner, who cast us all out of the garden!" He stood and raised his arms slowly until they were over his head. His fingers, then his hands, then his arms, jowls, and body began to shake with anger and, Nell supposed, the spirit.

Lewis stood too, with one hand on his pistol hip and one beady eye on the pastor. Nell took the men's lead and also stood, but she also grabbed the neck of the black bag. Whatever came next, Skully was staying with her. She kept an eye on the door and a hand on the bag as the red-faced pastor raged.

"More than any other daughter of Eve, more than any other person under the Kingdom of Heaven, Gunn Flagely hath wrought sin across the land! She brings Satan's corruption between her legs and lets it slip from her tongue like honey! And she writes *books*! Scientific books! About carnal matters!"

Nell was nearly dumbstruck. The pastor had a quite specific imagination regarding Gunn's anatomy. She wanted to hear what he said next, but Nell knew an opportunity when she saw one. While he was preaching against Gunn, she swiftly lifted her foot over the bench and made for the screen door behind her.

As she leaped from the porch and headed for the car in the barn, a loud bang rang out. She expected a hot bullet to rip through her flesh and shatter her tibia. No use stopping until she had to. She could hear her heart beating in her ears and her too-big leather shoes pounding the dry dirt—and then she could hear the heels of Lewis's cowboy boots and the *whap* of his holster against his thigh. He was right behind her, and his gun was holstered. The report she'd heard was the screen door slamming closed behind her. She slowed in relief.

"Go 'round!" Lewis breathed in her ear. He shoved the small of her back to get her back up to speed. "Go 'round!" he said again. "Get in the passenger side! Git! Git!" This time, the sound that rang out was indeed a shot, but it came from the porch where the old man was standing with a smoking rifle aimed in their direction. Lewis passed Nell with one hand holding his hat on his head and the other flinging open the driver's door.

Nell took Lewis's suggestion and threw herself onto the passenger seat. She reached for her flailing door as the man in the black hat threw the car into gear and stomped on the gas. They swung around in the dust and hightailed it back the way they'd come the night before as Nell finally swung her door closed.

Nell turned to see if anyone was following. No one was behind them yet, but they would be soon. The old man was chambering rounds in a long rifle and aiming at the car as it drove away. The men who had been at the breakfast table were running from the outbuildings toward the farmhouse.

It would be a minute or two before they could understand the old man's apoplectic ranting enough to get into vehicles and give chase. Now that the pastor had seen the skull with his own eyes, he was full of covetousness. There was no way he'd let it get away that easily.

Nell clutched the skull and looked at the man in the black hat with mouth agape. "What the hell was that?"

"Your friend's got quite a reputation," Lewis said. "Looks like Coyote's going back home." He nodded at the black bag. "It is old, right?"

"It's old," Nell acknowledged. "But without proper tools and a catalog and samples for comparison, I don't know how old."

"And it's Injun?"

"You know, it's funny you should ask that. I'm sure you're unaware, but that is actually a terrific question. You see, the American Indian tribes of the region have only been living in this area—"

"Don't matter. I'll just tell 'em it's one of theirs."

20

In Which Nell Nears the End

"Tell who it's one of theirs?" Nell demanded as the man in the black hat drove south. "Because whoever it is, Skully is not one of theirs. It is one of mine. It is mine."

"That skull is no more yours than it is anyone else's, Professor Kelly," said Lewis. "Unless you've got more money than an entire tribe of people. Then it can indeed be yours."

Nell hugged the skull inside its bag protectively. "A whole tribe? Which one?"

"Nez Perce. They've got bands all over the Wallowas. This whole area, including the mountains and the Snake River, was theirs for a long, long time."

"I know. I'm an anthropologist, not an idiot."

"Didn't say you were either. Just telling you who my next potential customers are."

"What happens after I tell these Indians what you want me to say, that it's one of theirs? They pay you, you throw

the money in the air and roll around in it like some kind of
evil, black-hatted, Wild West Jay Gatsby, and then what?
Will there be room for me in the car, or will it be filled to
the roof with cash? Will I have to walk back to Portland?
Are you going to shoot me?"

Lewis was silent.

"Well?"

He still said nothing.

"You're going to shoot me?!" Nell bolted upright in the
passenger seat, her eyes as huge as the car's headlamps.
"You said—"

"I'd rather not shoot you. I'm not a bounty hunter. I'm
a—" He looked into the air above his head to find the word
he wanted. "A procurer. And a damn good one. There's no
money on your head, just that guy's." He jerked a thumb
at the bag she held in her lap. "You're smart as a man, but
like most women, you talk a whole hell of a lot. You'll talk
somebody into getting you home, or a good way toward it."

"I'm as smart as anyone. End of sentence." Nell crossed
her arms and scowled out the window. They rode in silence
until they rejoined the road to Joseph at the junction in
Enterprise. The general store was open now, and the man
in the black hat slowed the car.

"You, uh, need any…"

"No," Nell said. "It was a ruse."

"Hm." The man in the black hat hit the gas again. "Didn't
work."

"It almost worked."

"But it didn't."

"Maybe if men weren't so afraid of women and their
menstrual cycles, you wouldn't get taken in like that.

I mean, it happens to half the world's population every month."

"But I didn't get taken in. I got you in the car before that infernal Gunn Flagely could catch us."

"After doing a little dance in the dirt, you did." Nell leaned across the seat to hiss in his ear, "You're squeamish."

"I am not. End of discussion."

Nell sat back, a smirk worthy of Gunn on her face.

The wheels in Nell's brain turned as quickly as the tires on the car. As they rolled toward Joseph, some twenty miles down the road, she said, "You said before that there's no money on my head."

"No, there is not," Lewis confirmed.

"How much money, exactly, is on Skully's head?" She took the skull from the bag and held it up, just as she had been holding it when she first met the man in the black hat and his pistol. It seemed eons ago, but it had only been a few days and one vast western state ago.

The man in the black hat hesitated. He glanced at her. He looked back at the landscape—nothing but fields full of wildflowers and granite, snowcapped mountains as far as the eye could see. Nell could almost hear the gears grinding as he calculated his risks. Finally he said, "Half a million dollars."

"Half a million?" Nell's eyes widened.

"That's the going price these days, from what I understand. Those monkey trials drove up the price for old skulls, especially on the black market. And especially the oldest skulls, which is what we all think you have in your hot little hand."

Nell whistled. "That is a lot of money. That would endow a whole anthropology department. Like the one we're trying to establish at the University of Oregon. You must know about that, though. That's how you found me. And him." She hefted the skull.

"I do. I can read newspapers."

"Thompson has a half million dollars easy."

"He does, that chicken-shit, skinflint bastard."

"Those weirdos in Paradise have a half a million dollars?"

"Oh, they got lots more than that. They call it a tithe; everyone else calls it a scheme. That farm's stuffed to the rafters with cash."

"The Nez Perce have that kind of money?"

"That one's a little trickier, but it's worth a try. If they all pool their beads and eagle feathers, they can probably meet my price. Or come close enough to get me rid of you." He thought a second, then went on. "If the Injuns absolutely cannot come close, it's on to some other rich bastard, those East Coast Astors and Carnegies and Rockefellers. They'll want something so rare, and they're willing to pay what I ask. Cash on the barrelhead. Whoever's able to plunk down that kind of cash will want an expert to verify what they're buying. You'll come in handy yet, Professor Kelly, one way or another."

A few miles later, a blink of an eye in sparsely populated eastern Oregon, they entered the fabled—to Nell, anyway—town of Joseph, former home of the oldest skull in North America, before it went on its whirlwind tour of the state. Lewis throttled the engine way back to crawl along the wide main street. It was the noon hour, and many horses and a few cars were lined up next to each other in front of stores and tack shops and garages—even a bronze foundry—for the three blocks that constituted downtown Joseph. A couple of cowboys stood next to their brown horses in the sun to watch the black car creep past. One of the cowboys, the shorter one, the one with splinters of sun shining through the curved brim of his straw hat and onto his adorable face, winked a blue eye at Nell as the car went by. Nell swallowed a gasp. *Casey.* He'd seen her.

They passed a church made of hewn tan stone blocks—the man in the black hat did not burst into flame, Nell noted—and the road made a sweeping curve to the left. The dark granite mountains that ringed the valley wore their white snow capes with pride, even in a late June heat wave. A grassy berm—actually, Nell thought, it was a moraine left behind by the glaciers that had carved the mountains and likely created a lake nearby—rose up between the road and the mountains as they came around the curve. A shiny black head popped up above the top of the rise as the car passed like a curious rock chuck. But this rock chuck slowly brandished a pistol in Nell's line of sight as a few other behatted or bare heads rose along the moraine. *That's the dig site,* Nell thought. *And they know we're here. Gunn knows we're here.* She tried not to squeeze the skull in her lap so hard she crushed it.

"If you break that skull," the man in the black hat said, "I will break yours. With a bullet."

Nell gulped and released her white-knuckled grip.

The Wallowa Mountain range had followed the road along her right and was now curling in front of the windshield. The car crept past a few women tending to a single gravestone at the side of the road.

"Who's that?" Nell asked.

"Old Chief Joseph."

"Of the Nez Perce?"

"The same."

"But the reservation is in Idaho, on the other side of these mountains."

"It is. That's why those local ladies have taken it upon themselves to keep up his grave. This was the summer camp of the Nez Perce for generations. Just because the government told them which piece of land was theirs don't mean they agree." He nodded in admiration as they drove along a long, calm, deeply blue-green lake at the base of the mountains and passed a lodge with little cabins arranged around it.

"Where are we going?" Nell asked as the lodge grew tiny in the rearview mirror until it was swallowed by the stately pine trees that grew like columns along the side of the road.

Lewis tossed his chin toward the mountains ahead. "There."

He pulled the car off the side of the road, which was now more of a groomed dirt trail, and came around to drag Nell out of the car. He grabbed her elbow but allowed her to carry the skull in its bag. Through the tall, skinny pines, Nell could make out another set of canvas tents and smell a fire burning. As they neared, she could see several people sitting near the tents and one tall, sharp-nosed man in denims and a snap-front shirt approaching them.

"Lewis," the man said in greeting.

"Jonathan," the man in the black hat returned.

Jonathan lifted his chin in Nell's direction and asked, "Who is she?"

"She's the scientist who can tell you if she holds Coyote's head in her hands."

Jonathan's gaze turned to the black bag. "Please," he said, gesturing toward the tents, "we would like to see our ancestor."

"Well, that's the thing," Nell began, "and it is an interesting thing—a fascinating thing, really, and quite a discovery—"

Lewis clamped down on Nell's arm, which also shut her mouth. "You got my money?" he asked Jonathan.

"We were not able to come up with all you asked, but all that we have is with us at the camp."

"How much is that?" Lewis asked with a suspicious eye.

"Three hundred seventy-five thousand American dollars, collected from tribes across the West. If the skull is as old as you say," he nodded at Nell, "it is an ancestor of us all."

"I haven't said a word about how old it is," Nell said, "and as a matter of fact—"

"She's a bit testy," Lewis explained as he thrust her forward to follow Jonathan to the camp. "You know women. Talk too much." He tapped her back with the snout of his pistol.

Filleted trout were arrayed around a pot of hot oil on a grill over the small fire, and the women were preparing dough to make fry bread. There were fewer than a dozen people in the camp, including a couple of children playing catch with a baseball and wearing leather mitts by the cold, fast-flowing river.

"You're here for summer hunting?" Nell asked. "Elk, I assume?"

"No," Jonathan said with a small smile and a shake of his head that sent his long, black hair quivering like feathers. He gathered it at his nape and twisted it into a loose, temporary rope. "We're on vacation, just like the white people in the park up the road. It's nice here. Even the white people like it. Not so much that they sleep in tents and listen to the river as they fall asleep; they've got that lodge on Wallowa Lake where my people used to set up the summer tepees. But we're happy out here in the trees too. Most of us work off the res in lumber and paper, so getting a week off to enjoy the trees instead of cutting them down and pulping them is a welcome change."

"I'd think you'd have had your fill of trees, working in the lumber industry," Nell said.

"No, never that," Jonathan said. "The smell of a paper mill, though—that a guy can fill up on real quick." He crouched and cleared pine needles and dried moss from a patch of dirt near the fire. He gestured for Nell to put the bag there.

She did, and she pulled open the drawstring and arranged the fabric away from the base of the skull. The contrast of the bone against the black bag made for a dramatic presentation, she thought. It made the skull seem worth a half a million dollars, even if it weren't the scientific breakthrough of phenomenal proportions she knew it to be.

Jonathan picked it up and held it to his face. Their noses would have been touching, if the skull had a nasal septum left. Jonathan and the skull looked deeply into each other's eyes.

"Now you tell me," he said to the skull, "how old are you, ancestor?"

"Well," Nell said, "that's what I've been trying to tell you. It is very old—probably, in all truth, the oldest skull ever found on this continent. I'll have to verify that in the lab, of course, but it really does seem like the real deal. Now, as for its being your ancestor, that's another fascinating question. You see, I—"

"You heard her," Lewis said. "The real deal."

Jonathan thought it over. "She also said she would have to verify it in the lab. I do not want to pay all the money of many impoverished tribes in order to keep someone's recently deceased uncle on a shelf in the reservation grange."

"Luckily, or obviously, the skull was found near here. Very near," Nell interjected. "There are scientists a few miles from here at the other end of the lake—"

"Iwetemlaykin," Jonathan said. "It is a sacred location. I have seen their tents and their digging." He did not seem impressed by the operation.

"Their grave robbing," said one of the other men quietly.

"If I could take this skull to the site, I could give you the best possible answer outside of a proper archaeological laboratory," Nell said without acknowledging their lack of respect for scientific discovery and rigor.

"Of course," said Jonathan as he stood.

"No way," said Lewis as he nabbed Nell's elbow. She was starting to develop contusions from the repeated force of his fingertips.

Jonathan eyed the man in the black hat carefully. "Why don't you want my people to learn the age of this skull?" The eyes of Jonathan's family, who had been listening as they cooked, peered at Lewis as well.

"That's not what I meant. It's…fine. Okay. Let's go see the eggheads." He led Nell back to the car, with Jonathan following closely, and a half dozen men from camp at his heels. The Nez Perce headed for two Model Ts parked near the tents. Jonathan was bringing backup, but Nell couldn't guess whose side they might be on in the showdown that was coming. Probably their own.

21

In Which the War for Skully Is Waged

The three-car caravan drove back down the road past the lodge, where guests were sunning themselves on the lawn; along the lake, which was dotted with fishermen in rowboats catching more rays than fish; and around the curve to the wide spot in the road at the base of the moraine.

"Here!" Nell said, pointing toward a flat piece of ground covered in stubbly, sunburned grass. Lewis swung the car left and stopped in a puff of dust.

The moraine loomed over them; on the other side of the sixty-foot berm, Nell knew, was Dr. Flagely's dig site. The two Model T cars carrying Jonathan and his cousins followed closely and chugged in beside Lewis's door.

The man in the black hat emerged first, surveying the moraine before him from behind his open door. As he looked left, back toward the lake, Gunn's head popped up on his right. Nell stepped from the car, the skull in its bag and both in her hand. She took a deep breath and waited for a signal. Would there be a signal? She had no idea. But a signal seemed to be something Gunn might give.

As the man in the black hat continued to look left, and Jonathan and his cousins emerged from their cars, Gunn's head dropped from sight. But Nell noticed a few other heads emerge to their left. There were a couple of tanned foreheads, likely grad students and archaeology amateurs who had come out to help Dr. Flagely at the site. There were also a couple of heads with knit caps flattened on them, even in the heat. She recognized one hat and pair of sparking eyes as belonging to one of the loggers she and Gunn had met at the general store in Mitchell. He raised a fist clenching a dull red cylinder, nodded, and sank below her line of sight. *Keep your friends close and the crazy guys with the TNT closer,* Nell thought as she sidestepped away from the open door of the car.

"Where are they?" the man in the black hat demanded. He apparently hadn't seen any of the heads popping up and disappearing over the moraine. Jonathan and his family were arranged behind him like a posse, with rifles held casually, as if they were twigs they'd cut from trees. The man in the black hat drew his own pistol and held it across the hood of the car in a less casual manner.

"The dig site is on the other side of the moraine," Nell said. It seemed silly to lie; she'd directed him to stop here.

"Who's Moraine?" sneered the man in the black hat.

"This big grassy thing," Nell said in exasperation. "Don't you live here?"

"I knew what it was," grumbled the cousin who had earlier complained about the grave robbing.

"We have to go over the moraine," Nell said loudly and clearly in the quiet morning, "and get to the tents Jonathan said he's seen over there. That will be the dig site, and there will be rudimentary tools and diagnostic materials that I can use to verify the age of this cranium."

"I will be so glad to be rid of you," rumbled the man in the black hat. "If it's leaving you out here in the middle of goddamn nowhere or killing you for whatever tiny mistake I can find."

"The feeling is mutual," said Nell. "Let's get this over with." She started directly up the moraine, veering slightly to the right, toward where she'd seen Gunn's glinting black bob. The men wound up a deer path that switchbacked among the lupines and forget-me-nots.

They'd only taken a few steps when another three cars tore around the curve and slammed on their brakes in the dusty makeshift parking lot. Clouds of dirt and dried grass flew up, making Nell sneeze. The pastor and his sons or workers or minions or flock or whatever the young men in tight jeans and checked shirts might be tumbled from their cars, guns at the ready. Nell was starting to miss her little pistol very much. She held the skull against her chest, not sure if she was protecting it or using it as her shield. Her very expensive, rare shield. She took backward baby steps up the moraine, sinking the heels of her brogues into the crumbly dirt and making her way Gunn-ward a couple of unnoticed inches at a time.

"What the hell are you doing here?" the man in the black hat said, drawing his second pistol and training it on the pastor. The boys in checkered shirts raised their rifles, and the Nez Perce men followed suit.

"You heathens and nonbelievers and evildoers have no moral authority over that skull. We have the voice of God and the hand of Jesus telling us that that skull is as full of lies as that woman's mouth." He flung a finger in Nell's direction, and she froze. None of the men bothered to look at her, though, and she continued her slow back-stepping up the moraine.

"That skull belongs to Coyote, the creator of our people and the founder of our tribes," said Jonathan. "It's older than any magical white man who can walk on water, and we aim to prove it."

"It don't matter what you all believe in," sneered the man in the black hat. "Like the rest of America, I believe in the almighty dollar, and that skull is worth more dollars than either of you are willing to put up. Maybe I'll just take it back myself, head east where the real moneybags live. I don't need either of you." He turned toward Nell and found her several feet above his head. "Where in the Sam Hill do you think you're going?" he yelled as he strode toward her with all the rifle-toting men in tow.

"Everyone else has a gun; why not Nell?" Gunn appeared on top of the moraine in her tweed and boots, pistol aimed between the eyes of the man in the black hat. It was enough of a vision to make the posse pause, which gave Gunn time to yell, "Now!"

The loggers stood up and lobbed their sticks of dynamite, now with sparking wicks, over the moraine without watching to see where the explosives landed. They all quickly dropped down while Nell scrambled up the rest of the steep slope and hid behind it next to Gunn. She landed on her belly, the skull at her side, just as the bombs exploded and exploded again, and the men let out a terrible yell. Nell peeked over the edge; the cars were ablaze and the men were scrambling up the grass, deer path be damned. As they reached the top, the grad students and volunteers set upon them with trowels, shovels, and wooden stakes of the kind that were usually used to rope off dig site sections close to the ground.

Gunn tugged on Nell's leather sleeve as the melee began and the dust rose and the grass flew. The two women crept down the moraine and toward a bank of trees at the edge of the large, flat expanse of meadow that stretched toward the Wallowa River at the base of the granite mountains. There were indeed white tents shading work tables and shallow trenches, but Nell wasn't going there. Gunn's hand at her elbow was guiding her toward the trees, where three horses with three riders waited. The rider in the middle was Casey. Nell felt relief and embarrassment and happiness rush over her. Not that she had time to deal with any one of those emotions, let alone all three.

"I'll catch up with you on the road, once I get these yahoos sorted and sifted," Gunn said with a jerk of her thumb toward the fracas on the moraine. She pressed the little pistol into Nell's hand, and Nell did not hesitate to tuck into the waistband of her dungarees. Gunn gave Nell a boost onto the chestnut horse ridden by Casey and slapped the mare on the rump to send it on its way. The horse merely trotted in place a little.

"You know that's not necessary," Casey said. "I've got the reins in my hand, and the horse can feel me on her back."

"You take all the drama out of a situation," pouted Gunn.

"When you're around, somebody has to," Nell said as Casey swung the horse around and headed toward Joseph.

"Won't be but a few minutes!" Gunn called after them.

As soon as the trees were behind them and there was open meadow ahead of them, the horses broke into a gallop. Nell tucked the skull between herself and Casey's back then held onto his waist for dear life. She didn't realize her eyes were squeezed so tightly closed until she opened them at the sound of the approaching Harley-Davidson. Right behind came another god-awful sound—the limping engine of the Pierce-Arrow. The loggers' dynamite had taken off the fabric-covered roof and the driver's side doors, plus put a hole in the hood that probably crippled the engine but hadn't put it out of its misery. The man in the black hat clutched the wheel and snarled. Nell waved to Gunn, who looked behind her. Then Gunn gripped her handlebars and grinned.

Gunn pulled her metal steed up next to Casey's mare, who did not spook in the least. Casey waved an arm at Gunn in her saddle, nodded toward Nell, and pointed down at the sidecar.

"You gotta jump," Casey yelled.

"You gotta be kidding me," Nell yelled back. Gunn just grinned up at them like she was having the time of her life. She probably was, Nell thought.

Gunn held the sidecar steady next to the horse, and Casey held out his left hand for Nell to use to steady herself in this death-defying rodeo stunt. Nell clutched the bag she'd been clutching for days that felt like a lifetime and swung her right leg to meet her left. She bounced with her belly on the saddle while sliding toward the sidecar. She took Casey's hand and lowered herself until her the tips of her brogues found the seat of the sidecar. She looked at Casey, who yelled "Now!" She let go of his hand and crouched in her sidecar. She swung her right hand with its precious cargo into the sidecar without it touching the ground. She tucked it in the nose of the sidecar, where she found her satchel, helmet, and goggles. She sat down and strapped her helmet and goggles into place as Gunn let out a whoop and saluted Casey. Gunn twisted her wrist and left the limping black car in the dust while the horses peeled off into a field at a gallop. Nell hunkered down and faced into the wind.

22

In Which Nell Confirms Her Suspicions

Gunn stopped only for gas as they barreled back to Eugene. By the time they arrived in the wee hours of the morning, Nell looked worse than anything any cat had ever dragged in. Gunn looked as if she had just emerged victorious from a hard-won battle with her lipstick as war paint. The motorcycle grumbled to a stop at the curb in front of Dr. Flagely's little house. Gunn led the way up the stairs, onto the porch, and through the front door, with Nell trailing in her wake like a tumbleweed being pulled along by a breeze.

Nell collapsed onto the velvet-covered divan, one leg not making it onto the furniture, one hand flung across her filthy, half-sunburned brow. For the first time in days, Nell released her grip on the sack that held the skull and let it rest on the Persian rug next to her.

"How did you know?" Nell asked quietly as Gunn passed through the living room.

"Know what?" Gunn paused.

"Where we were? That we were coming to Joseph?"

"My friend Wilma is Jonathan's cousin. Well, not cousin, but—it doesn't matter. She was in the camp down the road, with Jonathan. I was at the dig site with Daddy, and she came down to tell us that a man was on his way with their ancestor, Coyote. We went into town and called Casey, and one of the grad students drove hell for leather to find the loggers." Gunn's mischievous smile because wistful. "Wilma was so excited. It was such a long shot for the tribe." She paused again and looked at Nell. "You've got to give it back, you know. Ancestors mean so much to them."

"But the science… It's not… He's not…" Nell fell asleep before she could explain what she'd suspected from the first day she'd met Skully.

When Nell awoke, beams of light were streaming through the windows and her forearm was stuck to her forehead. She had opened her eyes at the sound of the Harley's rumbling engine, but she quickly realized the rumble had come from her own starving stomach. She sat up and blinked in the sudden sunlight. "Gunn?" she called, but she got no answer. The bath was clean and dry, the bedrooms were all empty, and Gunn was long gone.

Nell shuffled into the kitchen and started a pot of coffee and some hot water for oatmeal. There wasn't even a dish in the sink; Gunn hadn't eaten here. Nell surmised that the woman had taken a bath and gone out again while Nell had slumbered so deeply that she'd noticed neither the roar of the engine nor the truly uncomfortable position she'd landed in on the divan.

Nell checked the front porch for a newspaper and found two folded on the doormat. The motorcycle was no longer at the curb where she'd stumbled away from it the night before. Gunn had even taken Nell's goggles and helmet, Nell realized with a bit of nostalgia. She brought both papers in and realized she'd missed an entire day. No wonder she was so sore. She looked at the clock on the wall—nine o'clock. She sipped her coffee and ate her oatmeal. She washed her dishes and then decided to wash herself—thoroughly. It wasn't going to be a bath; it was going to be a lesson in gross anatomy.

She started the water and kicked off her dusty old brogues. She removed her crusty dungarees and her stained jersey. She'd managed to toss the leather jacket over the back of Dr. Flagely's desk chair the night they'd arrived. Dark-brown dirt and pinkish, suntanned skin ringed her wrist and made a shallow V at her throat. Her hair was a cloud of blond curls that might never see anything like sleek again, if they ever had. The freckles on her nose and cheeks, she saw in the mirror, were unspeakably brown, and in the pale swath across her forehead, where her helmet had protected her from the sun, there was a bright-red kiss planted like a third eye. She'd even slept through that.

When she finally emerged after remaining in the bath for a nearly Gunn-worthy forty-five minutes, Nell wrapped herself in a towel and went to the room that would have been hers, if all had gone according to plan. Which it had very much not. The dress she had been wearing the day she'd arrived in Eugene was laid out neatly on the bed with a note:

Daddy says you should meet him at the university cafeteria for brunch. Bring Skully.
— *GF*

Her heeled shoes were paired on the floor below the dress's hem, and a fresh tube of magenta lipstick was tucked into her little purse. It was a bolder color than Nell would ever pick for herself, but after dressing and combing her hair into an approximation of a neat bob, the new paint seemed just right against her tanned and freckled skin.

Nell's still-growling stomach told her that a second round of breakfast would be most welcome. And after all this time, she would finally meet the esteemed Dr. Flagely.

Nell found Dr. Flagely and what appeared to be a student of his at a table in the center of the cafeteria. She loaded her tray with eggs, potatoes, toast, butter, and sausage, plus a mug of strong Oregon coffee. She was pleased to see that the professor and his student had a pot to themselves in the middle of the table. She placed Skully in his worn, filthy bag next to it.

"Dr. Flagely. I am honored to finally meet you." Nell stuck out her hand. Dr. Flagely stood to shake it.

"Well done, Professor Kelly," Dr. Flagely said. "I am honored to meet a colleague brave enough to chase down a stolen archaeological find—and endure my daughter and her infernal motorcycle machine." Dr. Flagely introduced his student assistant, Mabel.

"How did you get back to Eugene so quickly?" Nell asked the professor.

"You mean without my demon daughter at the wheel?" Dr. Flagely chuckled. "I had a larger engine, a larger gasoline tank, and Mabel here, who shared time behind the wheel. There are sensible ways to travel quickly. We arrived this morning. I've only had time to drop some things off in my office and come here for some much-needed nourishment."

Nell swallowed a forkful of food and leaned closer to the professor. "Any sign of the man in the black hat?"

"Not a peep," said Dr. Flagely. "His car gave up the ghost between Joseph and Enterprise, and none of his new friends felt any obligation to stop and help. Not even those Christian folks." He shook his head in amused dismay. "His Nez Perce friends merely walked back to camp, none the poorer, except for the need to buy a couple of replacement Model Ts. The pastor and his boys headed back to whatever circle of hell they inhabit. And your friend in the black hat, last I saw him, was shooting his dead car and cursing your name."

Nell smiled. "With a few unrepeatable phrases before and after, I assume."

"He was saying 'professor' as if it were a curse word itself." He chuckled again and looked at Mabel. "The students have the impression that archaeology is always that exciting. Poor children."

"I hope it's never that exciting for me again," Nell said as she refilled her coffee cup. "Now that we've got the skull back, where shall I take it? I'm ready to begin the work I came here for, even if I am two weeks late in getting started."

"You can take it to the newly very securely locked chemistry lab," said Dr. Flagely. "Mabel here will be your assistant,

Miss Kelly, while you work on your new dating technique. She is very good with bones."

Mabel beamed. "I'm hoping to be in the first class to graduate from the University of Oregon with a proper anthropology degree. I've had to make do studying natural science so far, but Dr. Flagely has helped a great deal." She was only a couple of years younger than Nell, who wondered if she'd seemed that freckle-faced and innocent her first summer in the field. Probably; after all, Gunn had thought her freckle-faced and innocent just last week when Nell stood in the doorway of Mohle House. Nell may have lost some of her innocence, but the eastern Oregon sun had brought out a slew of new freckles that no amount of Max Factor makeup could conceal.

"Where is Gunn?" Nell asked as she cut a fresh piece of sausage and loaded her fork.

"She was out all night at some fraternity party on campus, and she went back to Portland this morning. She was only supposed to escort you to the lab in the first place, not go gallivanting all over the state on that dadblasted Harley-Davidson with a visiting professor thrown in the sidecar." He shook his head, but his dismay seemed an attempt to hide his pride. "Any excuse for an adventure, that girl."

"I'm an ivory tower girl myself. Adventure isn't really my area of expertise." Nell smiled, but it felt as painted on as her lip color. As the three of them finished their meals with gusto, they gossiped about the anthropological world, including the latest scuttlebutt on Margaret Mead. Nell wasn't the gossiping type, but she was as hungry for academic conversation as she was for her breakfast.

"Well, shall we get to work?" She looked at the professor

and his protégé as they let their forks clatter to their empty plates.

"We shall, we shall," Dr. Flagely said. He led the two young women to what would someday, with the help of Nell Kelly, become the anthropology department.

Nell and Mabel worked long hours in the chemistry lab for three weeks, well into the dry heat of July. Every evening when she left the lab, Nell waited for a thunderstorm to break the heat, but it never came. There was no humidity in the air, only unrelenting sunshine followed by cool, starlit nights. Her dorm room had an electric fan, but it was little help, even when she gave in and lounged in her cotton slip while studying the latest research in osteology. And the occasional monograph by renowned sexologist Gunn Flagely, which she kept hidden under her thin mattress. At least she had her trunk now and a few changes of clothes. No dusty dungarees for days on end.

By the end of that overly hot summer, Nell had confirmed what she had suspected all along, what she had tried to tell everyone between Eugene and Joseph, if they hadn't kept cutting her off every time she talked. She strode into Dr. Flagely's office with a thick stack of typed pages in her hands and Mabel trailing in her wake. Nell hadn't been in this office since the man in the black hat had plucked her quiet summer right from the palm of her hand. She couldn't help but glance around cautiously as she approached the desk, where Dr. Flagely sat with a proud smile. She dropped the pages in front of him with a smack.

"You seem happy," Dr. Flagely said. "You confirmed your suspicions?"

"I confirmed three things," Nell began. She held her hand in the air and lifted a finger for each point. "First, chemistry can be helpful in determining age; as chemistry discovers more properties of radioactive elements, it can only benefit archaeology. Details of my theory are in my paper. But for now, it is only slightly better than the comparison methods we've been using for decades.

"Second, this is indeed the oldest skull found in the New World, undoubtedly. The shape of the cranium and the development of the molars and jaw tell us that. Also, the strata at which it was buried is deeper than any other known burials in the Northwest; Franz Boas has confirmed that via letters to me.

"And third," Nell paused dramatically, three fingers held aloft. Mabel held her breath in anticipation, though the girl had typed the pages on the desk and so knew what was coming. "Third, it is not a Nez Perce ancestor. It is definitely not Coyote. It is not even a Native American skull. I believe," she paused again to savor Dr. Flagely's expectant expression, "that this is the skull of a man who traveled from Southeast Asia."

Dr. Flagely's jaw dropped. Mabel's delicate hands flapped together like a hummingbird clapping. "Are you sure?" the professor asked.

"As sure as I can be with the tools and data available. This skull," she put her palms on the desk and leaned in, her magenta lips curled in a catlike smile, "would be worth many, many millions of dollars to collectors. It is so rare and so important as to be beyond monetary calculations in the scientific community. And certainly it will shore up the establishment of a very, very active archaeology department. And cultural anthropology," she added.

Dr. Flagely stood behind his desk and clapped. Mabel fluttered her hands together again. Nell basked in their attentions.

"Of course, the Nez Perce will be quite disappointed," Dr. Flagely said.

"He wasn't buried with any native burial goods, and he seemed to have fallen where he was, according to your photographs and data," Nell said. "All known native artifacts—arrowheads, pot sherds, fire pit remnants—were at least one strata above these remains. His teeth are worn in ways unlike the remains of known native peoples. He was here first. He beat old Christopher Columbus and any adventurous Vikings. Besides," she went on, "the shape of his mandible points to ancient Asiatic heritage. On its own, that fact is not definitive, but with the dental clues, I believe I am correct."

"Extraordinary," Dr. Flagely said. "This will of course have to be vetted by a board of your peers before it can be published."

"I'm confident in my findings and will defend my thesis."

"If it is even plausible, if the science is solid—"

"It is."

"Then we'll publish it and present it at the university's fiftieth anniversary in October. Will you be able to stay for the ceremony?"

"I'll be back at Barnard teaching Intro to Archaeology and continuing my work on my paper, which stars old Skully," Nell said. "I've got more to do regarding the chemistry of remains and surrounding soils. And I've got to mothball that whole dendrology idea for skeletal remains. There's got to be a connection between bone decay and atomic decay, and I want to find it."

"You are a very driven woman, Miss Kelly," Dr. Flagely said with a shake of his head.

"She certainly is," Mabel said, her hands clasped in front of her heart.

Nell defended each and every point of her thesis to the satisfaction of the professors at the University of Oregon at the conclusion of her residency in August. She also defended herself against the old-fashioned ideas of the panel.

"Very nice work, Miss Kelly," said one of the three men who sat at the table before her. He took off his wire-rimmed glasses and rubbed his brow, then sat back in his chair. The official part of the defense had concluded. "I assume you're going Back East soon?"

"Yes, sir. I still have much work to do on the chemical component of dating remains, as you read in my paper."

"Yes, yes," he said. "But you'll probably be happier to see your beau after a summer away than to shut yourself up in a lab again."

Nell's brow knotted in confusion at this conversational turn. "I have no beau."

"No beau?" asked another of the professors. "You must have someone by now, at your age." He hastily added, "And for being so lovely."

Nell stood erect and smoothed her skirt. "I am headed Back East to Barnard College and, with any luck, Columbia University in New York City. I will indeed shut myself off in a lab again, as soon as I leave Grand Central Station. You may be surprised, gentlemen, to learn that some women have ideas in their brains and not just babies on their minds. Any man who wants to take even a modicum of my time has to understand that he will never get all of my time. That man may be out there, but I have yet to meet him." She slid the strap of her beat-up leather satchel over her shoulder. "I was going to say that this wasn't any of your business, but being professors, it is exactly your business. I am not the first and I will not be the last woman who stands before you to defend her thesis. She should not also have to defend her sex or her choices in life. Thank you so much for your time and consideration." Nell gave a curt nod and walked from the dim room into the bright, hot Oregon sunshine.

The next morning, Nell took the train from Eugene to Portland, a mere three-hour ride in a proper seat with scenery passing outside the window. She might miss Oregon's snowcapped mountains and the clear air and the lava beds, but she would never miss having her teeth rattled out of her gums in that sidecar.

She arrived at Union Station just before noon; the Empire Builder didn't leave for Chicago until about four. Since she had a cross-country ticket, the attendants were kind enough to take her bag and trunk into their care while she hopped onto the streetcar to Mohle House. She crossed the river and hopped off the streetcar at Thirty-Fourth and Belmont, then walked the two blocks to the steep concrete steps leading to the porch of the dark-red house, her satchel swinging against her hip.

She knocked on the door and was greeted by a flurry of silken fabric and long strands of pearls flying toward her—and glasses framing the dark, shining eyes.

"Nell!" Gunn flung her long arms around Nell, nearly knocking them both off balance. Gunn regained her footing first and grabbed Nell's hand to drag her into the study with the fireplace and the piles of paper on every surface. "I've been hard at work ever since we got back, as have you, Daddy says. Of course, I'm just cataloging a selection of animist fertility goddess sculptures for an exhibit at the Met; you were making history. But the show is set to open in September, and I made a bit of a mess for myself in taking off to eastern Oregon like that. It's not like I didn't know I had the Met on the line." She gestured at the tipsy piles of photographs and note cards prepared to become an avalanche of information at the slightest tremor of the floorboards.

Of course she's mounting an exhibit at the Metropolitan Museum of Art, Nell thought. *Of course she raced off on her motorcycle rather than working on a show for one of the most important museums in the country.* Nell's mind treaded water briskly enough to keep her out of the morass of jealousy. She had just identified the oldest skull in the country. She had a manuscript being published in the fall and a letter of recommendation for full professorship from one of the most acclaimed archaeologists to the finest anthropology school in America, if not the world. She had helped establish an archaeology department at a university on the opposite side of the continent. She had outfoxed the bad guy. She had been kidnapped once, maybe twice if you count Gunn and the sidecar, and held at gunpoint more times than she'd like to remember. She straightened her posture.

"An exhibit at the Met? That's wonderful," she said.

The pocket door leading to the dining room slid open, and a tall, thin blond man with a sheet wrapped around his carved-ivory waist stepped halfway into the room. "Sorry to interrupt, ladies, but I was going to take a bath. I know, it is awfully late in the day to be getting around to one's bath, but we've been, well, busy." He leered at Gunn, who leered right back through her lenses. "Do either of you need to use the facilities first?"

"No, thank you," Nell said, though she didn't know why anyone who walked around with a sheet around his waist would be shy and gracious about taking a bath.

"That reminds me," Gunn said to Nell, "did you ever find Casey again?"

"I didn't look," Nell said. "I was in the lab, and then I had to finish the paper with the proof. Casey was out riding fences or whatever it is cowboys do. He didn't even send a letter. Besides, I was really happy while I worked. I can't imagine Casey being glad to have a lover who worked all day in a lab and collapsed into bed with a scientific journal at night. I don't cook, I don't clean, and I don't care to ever learn to do either."

"Well, that's too bad. About Casey, not about your work. About that I'm just as pleased as rum-spiked punch." She held Nell's chin in her hand and pinned Nell's gaze with her sparkling, dark eyes. "Don't you ever learn to cook, Nell Kelly."

"I promise I never will." Nell smiled. "I'm sorry this visit has to be so short, but I need to catch a trolley back to the station so I don't miss the train."

"Of course," Gunn said as she walked Nell to the door. "You want a ride? One last time in the sidecar?"

"No!" Nell said too quickly. "Thank you."

"I see you stole one of our satchels." Gunn eyed the bag at Nell's hip.

"Oh! I'm sorry. I didn't mean…if you want…"

Gunn punched Nell in the arm, which hurt. "Don't be a fluffy bunny. Of course you can have it. Adventurers require sturdy satchels."

"Thank you," Nell said again.

Gunn smiled. "I'll look you up next month when I'm in New York at the Met."

"You will not."

"I will! We can go dancing."

Nell's wide eyes betrayed her terror, which only made Gunn smile wider. Gunn opened the door, and Nell stepped onto the porch.

"Thanks for…" Nell trailed off.

"Magenta paint looks good on you," Gunn said. "Sets off your tan." She waved and shut the door, and Nell traipsed down the stairs and to the trolley stop. This color of lipstick did look good on her.

When she reached Union Station for the last time, Nell retrieved her bags, punched her ticket, and settled into her seat on the train. At precisely 4:30 p.m., the train's engine pulled it forward and the whistle sounded. She watched Portland slowly pull away. The conductor came around a few hours later to call everyone to dinner, and Nell stood to make her way to the dining car. She wasn't very hungry; her stomach felt as if it had sad butterflies inside it. She took a seat at a table for two and waited for her dinner partner. She hoped it was a deaf old man so they could eat in silence, but it wasn't. It was a young man with reddened, leathery hands and a straw cowboy hat that had spent a summer fading under the sun to pale gold.

"Glad to see you're well, Professor Kelly," said Casey. "Last time we met, you were climbing off my horse and into the sidecar of that Harley. That was a stunt worthy of the riders at the Pendleton Round-Up."

"What are you doing here?" Nell asked in pleasant shock.

"I've got to get Back East, same as you," he answered with a smile. He removed his hat and placed it on the bench beside him.

"Montana isn't Back East."

"Nope," he said. "I'm working on my mineralogy doctorate at Penn and teaching geology classes."

"Mineralogy?"

"Study of minerals. It comes in handy in the mining business," Casey confirmed.

"I know what it is," Nell said. "At Penn?"

"University of Pennsylvania. In Philadelphia."

"I know where it is," Nell said.

"All the way Back East. Changing trains in Chicago."

"Me too. Then I go on to—"

"Barnard College in New York City. Maybe even Columbia University. I know. Everyone across the whole state of Oregon knows that by now, Professor Kelly. You're nearly as famous as Gunn Flagely, thanks to Skully and that motorcycle ride to recover him. This'll give us a couple thousand miles to get to know one another without any outlaws on your tail or whiskey in your veins. Unless you want whiskey in your veins?" Casey grinned and shook his little flask.

"Maybe later," Nell said, "if you don't mind the fact that I always have bones on the brain."

"Don't mind at all, if I can bend your ear about some mineral studies I'd like to do while I've got the university's laboratory facilities at my disposal."

"Don't mind at all." Nell smiled. "I'll even allow you to buy me a steak with the money you made this summer. A university stipend doesn't stretch very far. I'm afraid I'm broke."

"Don't mind at all, Nell Kelly. Don't mind at all."

The End

CPSIA information can be obtained
at www.ICGtesting.com
Printed in the USA
FFOW02n1156230518
46820390-48992FF